The Tail of the Flaming Lion and Other Such Tales

BY MARK VAN HOUTEN

Dorrance Publishing Co
585 Alpha Drive
Pittsburgh, PA 15238
Visit our website at *www.dorrancebookstore.com*

ISBN: 979-8-8872-9229-8
eISBN: 979-8-8872-9729-3

The Tail of the Flaming Lion
and Other Such Tales

Dedication

This book is dedicated to my mother, Lillian; to my wife of forty-six years, Leslie; and to my three grandkids, Olivia, Madison and Emma, to whom I read these stories.

Table of Contents

The Love Letter

"Get out of the way, Billie," demanded one of the testy prison guards, as she jangled the jail keys and flung open the gate. "Here's your new roomie. You'll be sharing this cell with Elliot for a while, 'til we get him settled."

Spoiling his pretty-boy face, Billie flared his nostrils, scrunched his tight lips, shook his coiffed blond ringlets, and unleashed his pent up arrogance by shouting, "What? Who is this piece of shit?"

A small, impish prisoner edged into the cramped cell: a cold, dank, and decaying encasement, drenched in artificial light and infused with a whiff of rotting pine, mingling with the nasty stench of moribund prior occupants. The queer little man wandered to a narrow corner wedged between a bed and sink. He sat on the floor and squeezed his folded knees against his chest. The glare of the piercing ceiling lights illuminated his sullen complexion, peppered with teardrop tattoos. His squinty, evasive eyes, snide snout, and sharp jaw wrinkles exuded the caricature of a spoor hungry rodent with a remorseless demeanor, in Billie's opinion. The tally marks scarring Elliot's forearm caused Billie concern.

"Officer," voiced Billie with steaming vitriol. "This guy looks like some mangy weasel. Put him in a cage, but not in my cell."

The officer, moving to exit, turned and said to Billie sarcastically, "Try to be civil."

Billie pivoted to Elliot and laid down the law. "Look, buddy, you stay on your side, and I'll stay on mine. That's my bed, and that one's yours. You can tell which sink is mine by looking at my wall mirror."

Billie elevated his entire arm with theatrical flair to trace the borders of his own reflection in the mirror. As he framed his image with an extended finger, he drew attention to a bevy of beautifully scripted correspondence letters, each suspended from a long plastic cord fastened to the outer edges of the mirror, the design fashioned to resemble a holy tabernacle. Billie took a moment to pose his handsome, faux debonair face and sleek, sexy physique at the center of the testimonial display.

"See, Elliot," said Billie, while admiring his trademark veneer reflected in the obedient mirror. "Each of these is a love letter from one of my forever sweethearts. After all these years they are all still infatuated with me, despite the fact that I jilted each one of those whores out of a fortune; fools they were and still are." Billie snorted triumphantly. He continued, "Only one bitch caught me and prosecuted. I was sentenced to ten years, but I'll be out in two, thanks to my loophole-clever legal team. Once out, I'll claim my just desserts, and maybe juice up some new lucrative passions again."

"What about you, Elliot? What are you in for?"

Elliot's fangs growled in response. "None of your fucking business!"

Billie chuckled. "All right, caveman. Go ahead and mount YOUR love letters on YOUR mirror." Elliot scowled and looked away.

"What's the matter?" queried Billie with a snickering click of his tongue. "What, no love letters, no fan club? Ahhh, so sad." Billie gloated patronizingly, but then launched into, "I'll make you a deal. I'll gift you one of my love letters, if you tell me what landed you in the slammer." Billie reached down under his mirror to a collection of as yet unopened envelopes.

"Here. Elliot, have a good time on me. Pick one of mine and pretend it's for you." Elliot eyeballed the scatter of envelopes. He used the arm incised with scarred tally marks to pick the one standout envelop in bright pink, caressed with a lipstick kiss.

"Okay, Elliot. You like the pink one? Here, you can have it. It's from a…ah…Elizabeth Tippen." Billie's forehead furrowed quizzically. "I don't recognize the name. Maybe a new recruit." Billie shrugged, then flapped the letter under Elliot's nose, saying, "Here, she's yours. Now confess your crime."

Elliot took the letter without uttering a word, so Billie insisted impatiently, "Okay, now, what's YOUR crime, buddy?"

"Fuck you, and get out of my face," scoffed Elliot, who tore open the envelop and read its contents silently under Billie's curious gaze, chin up, neck strained, and eyes bugged out. With the letter read and clenched in his grinning teeth, Elliot slinked off to another corner of the cell, and started masturbating vigorously, yipping like a dog in celebration. Billie's pristine veneer crumpled.

"What's in that letter? Let me see it!" Billie swiped to grab it, but Elliot lurched away, shielding the letter from Billie's reach.

"I'll tell you tomorrow, asshole."

•   •   •   •   •

Billie couldn't sleep that night. Tossing and turning, his curiosity about the letter's contents ate at his gut. *After all, the letter was meant for me alone.* Finally, he could no longer resist his jealous impulses. He snuck over to Elliot's corner. Picked up the letter. Pealed back the envelop leaf, and eased the letter out slowly so as to not awaken Elliot.

Okay. What's this Tippen thing all about? whispered Billie, lips curled at the edges, eyes in titillation mode.

The letter read: THIS IS THE NIGHT YOU DIE, MOTHERFUCKER, signed Elizabeth Tippen.

TEN, ELEVEN, TWELVE: Justin imagines himself a winged, transmogrified, celestial spirit, white and pure, hovering next to Jesus at the altar.

THIRTEEN: Justin poses as God's altar boy. *To you I raise my head. Close my eyes. Open my mouth. Offer out my tongue.*

FOURTEEN.

The End

How Not To
Treat Your Alien

Chapter One

It was an awesome sight to behold. Revealing itself, like the gaping maw of a cornucopian cavern framed by undulating filigrees of swirling, twirling grey and amber cosmic gas clouds, the massive wormhole swallowed the western morning sky over Central Command. Billions of years since God's light created a presumably anthropocentric universe, this ominous darkness from across the cosmos of all creation now eclipsed humanity's parochial isolation. August 1st, a momentous day in history, human or otherwise.

Waves of sparkling galactic dust poured out from within the wormhole and wend its way gently and ever downward to the receiving platform, no more than a few hundred feet from the welcoming party. Earnest, the senior staff counsel, and his colleagues, the best of humanity's philosophers, scientists, and politicians, stared intensely in utter amazement at the reconstituting spacecraft, as it materialized from the chalky wake of apparent nothingness.

The welcoming party consisted of twelve officials from the International Organization of Extra-Terrestrial Manifestations. Earnest was appointed as the chief spokesperson, due to his singularly piercing intellect and deep respect for all life forms. Standing tall with waving grey hair and waxed mustache, Ernest exuded both a commanding presence and open curiosity in a rare mix of diplomat and scientist.

Ernest had championed attempts to communicate between Earth and any intelligent extraterrestrial life, when such attempts were greeted with ridicule. His first success was contact with Quintilian b, which orbits an M-type red dwarf star in the constellation Orion, a mere 4.2 million light years from earth. Quintilian b sits between two immensely powerful black holes, Sagittarius A* and Messier 87. Amazingly, the Quintilians had harnessed the power of Dark Energy infusing vacuum space, and, consequently, the space/time warp between massive black holes, to create a slick space-time portal. For the Quintilians, the transit time from home to Earth was a mere two Earth weeks. The committee was witnessing the maiden voyage of an alien life form to the planet Earth. No one knew what to expect. "I've never met an intelligent extraterrestrial creature," murmured the committee members in great anticipation. Craig, the military attaché, was not so much enthused.

On this maiden flight, the Quintilians were represented by OoPjf-137d, who was their sole ambassador of communication between the two life forms. OoPjf-137d's visit was authorized by a new H-1B visa status, devised specifically to authorize interplanetary exchanges of extraterrestrials. To qualify for the H-1B program, an alien must demonstrate proficiency in a human language.

OoPjf-137d hailed from an advanced tribe of Quintilians that occupied the planet's narrow, equatorial band, the so-called Terminator Line, where the Habitable Zone's atmosphere is not too thin so as to permit respirations and even phonation. OoPjf-137b had mastered English quite well, but it was feared that his vocalizations in Earth's atmosphere might be poorly stabilized and thus migrate unexpectedly over extreme ranges of pitch frequencies, thus creating bizarre harmonic overtones and tempos, rendering human interpretation of his verbal nuance, if based solely on speech intonation, very challenging, and even confusing, for humans. Since the Quintilians had developed more subtle forms of direct mind-to-mind communication, they assumed that a glitch in this more humanoid form of communication would be of little consequence.

The vacuum-sealed hatch of the space-time module opened with a decompression "whoosh." Peeking through, a single long, dark tendril emerged and touch-crept along the smoothly glistening outer shell of the craft. Soon, other creeping tendrils were visible, each coated with a fuzzy mat of hairy spines and barbs. The tendrils converged on a central core, looking like an amorphous globule with a bubbling surface of oblong pseudopodia, seeming to scope out the terrain.

Now fully erect, OoPjf-137d was an imposing figure, rising to several feet over the tallest in the committee. As its torso unfolded, a plethora of undulating tendrils emerged, each wriggled serpentine-like in advance of the creature's forward locomotion. One could envision how these tendrils made it possible for Quintilians to navigate over the vertical cliffs and rocky terrain that was home to these creatures.

"Look at those appendages," whispered Craig to the other members of the welcoming committee. "Do you think he could play for the NBA?" Giggling spread among the members like wildfire. "I wonder what he's like on the dance floor." The giggling became audible.

In advance of the welcoming committee, the press corps surged the landing platform, shouting out questions, like, "Did God make you in His image?"

Truth be told, early contacts between earthlings and Quintilians sought common philosophic grounds. Since Quintilians were also God-fearing people, attempts by religious authorities on both sides sought to bring together the God of the Quintillians and the God of the Earthlings. The failure of this project on multiple occasions was attributed speculatively to ineffective prayer communication protocols. Others speculated that each God governed a different Universe in the Multiverse, so they may not know of each other. Nonetheless, work on this project continued in earnest, due to strong public support on both sides.

Earnest commanded the reporters to step aside and let the creature descend. OoPjf-137b splayed its panoply of long sinuous tendrils, inching along the slick surface of the space module, but there were no supports. With no grips, OoPjf-137d slipped off the platform, careened down the stairs toward the tarmac, and made a hard landing in a slimy puddle of jet fuel and solid seepage from the water closet drain. Aghast, the welcoming committee dropped their jaws, except for Craig, the military attaché, whose restrained giggles burst into barking guffaws.

"This is hysterical!" wriggled Craig, who could not catch his breath between bursts of laughter. All gazed in awe as the creature's oblong projections bubbled up and down in all directions erratically from its central globule.

"Oops, here I am. Spaceman at your service," burst Craig rudely, while aping the creature's comic flop.

Earnest leapt to his feet and pivoted to address the rowdy crowd. "Can't you see he is embarrassed?" intervened Earnest, appealing to human sensitivities. OoPjf-137d regained his composure, and awkwardly approached the committee.

"Hello, my name is OoPjf-137d," announced the alien in a harshly grating voice. "The Central Command of Quintilian b sent me to you, our closest intergalactic neighbor, to notify you earthlings about an existential threat to both our civilizations."

Craig just could not resist the invitation to mock the gangly alien again. "Do you mind if we call you 'Oops' for short?" Again, the giggling was irrepressible. Earnest waved off the ridicule.

OoPjf-137d unfurled a fuzzy tendril, which he directed to the eastern horizon. "I come to deliver a dire warning to the aliens of Earth. Dark Energy is expanding and tearing apart our universe with alarming speed, as Intergalactic Dark Gravity is weakening. Soon, stars and galaxies will be too far away to see them. Then, all matter will be rent apart. To prevent a catastrophic disintegration of our sister galaxies, our scientists and yours must work together in common cause."

Earnest stepped forward from the stunned crowd and extended his hand to OoPjf-137d in a gesture of universal friendship. The alien latched onto Earnest's arm firmly with a hairy tendril, which edged upward along his forearm. Earnest could feel the tingly-prickly sensation of the tendril's bristles on his exposed flesh, digging in and infusing his body with electric pulsations. As in a flash on the inside of his eyelids Ernest saw a holographic scene from the surface of Quintilain b. Creatures just like OoPjf-137d were climbing along the deeply scored caverns of the Habitable Zone, where they were protected from the flares of high-emission stellar winds spewing from the red dwarf star and strafing the exposed surface of the planet. While Earnest was mentally distracted, OoPjf-137d's power of telepathic communication entered Earnest's brain and scoured his mind for clues. The invasive tendril could feel benevolent impulses radiating from Earnest's mind, providing OoPjf-137d with an intuition that Earnest was curious and possibly open to accepting the alien race. OoPjf-137d's telepathic antennae knew that Earnest could be trusted.

Chapter Two

Earnest and the committee escorted OoPfj-137d into the main terminal, where they were confronted by an urgent messenger sprinting from Central Command to announce breathlessly, "There's an asteroid racing on a collision course with the Earth! Expect impact in twelve hours. Best projections are that it will hit the massive waterway just north of us." Earnest knew that this main river channel bifurcated into a pair of outflowing rivers. A powerful hit might create a thousand-foot wall of water, a massive tsunami, propagating upstream to the bifurcation point. Fortunately, each outflow river was restrained by a dam. Yet a massive tsunami could destroy one or both and drown the inhabitants downstream.

Earnest inquired of the messenger about the downstream status of each river. "One branch leads to the Astronomical Institute, which houses our elite league of scientists. The other river leads to a small settlement of wayward recluses, some kind of a religious cult, devoted to the worship of whatever."

Thinking strategically, Earnest reasoned, if one of the dams were to burst prematurely, then the tsunami could be diverted away from those downstream from the intact dam. But which dam should be protected, and which exposed?

"You must detonate and destroy the dam feeding the settlement," urged the messenger frantically. "Our scientific team at the Astronomical Institute has some of our most elite minds and must be protected above all, even if it means sacrificing a bunch of nut jobs."

The messenger drew Earnest aside to reveal top-secret documents showing that scientists at the Institute had been working on a method of altering the course of rogue asteroids that could threaten the Earth. They published that a pre-emptive strike on any such asteroid could deflect it in any direction desired. Unfortunately, THIS very asteroid was completely uncharted and unknown to its scientists. Thus, it was too late to alter its course. Collision could not be averted. Earnest suspected that something or someone must have drawn this asteroid out of its orbit.

"I'll bet it was drawn out by the wormhole that Oops used for space/time travel," asserted Craig firmly. "We know nothing of its potential to alter forces within our universe, and the Quintillians are capable of using Dark Energy to attack us in our ignorance." The committee members were alarmed by Craig's conspiratorial claims and called for OoPjf-137d to stand trial.

Craig stood at attention and proclaimed, "To hell with intergalactic Racial Justice. We need to drill Oops about this wormhole, and whether there is a conspiracy to render Earth vulnerable to attack…. By the way, where is Oops?" The technician retorted, "The alien was here just a moment ago, now he's gone. We need to find him immediately."

Meanwhile, Earnest faced a difficult decision. Both populations were at risk for annihilation by the tsunami wave, unless one of the dams was destroyed in advance. A fierce debate broke out amongst the committee members, including the on-site Ethicist. Speculation was rife that Oops had colluded with his allies on Quintilian b to divert an asteroid to Earth specifically to create chaos and havoc, perhaps in preparation for an invasion of Earth.

Persuaded by the mounting paranoia, Earnest ordered the bombing of the dam that shielded the settlement and directed a rescue team to pick up the scientists at the Institute, just in case.

Meanwhile, Oops re-entered in his wormhole, and dialed it back two days in time to face the Astronomical Institute on an urgent fact finding mission.

Chapter Three

The languid late summer sky at dusk over the Astronomical Institute on July 30th seemed peaceful enough, until it was rent open in a blazing flash by the glittering outline of a massive wormhole, exploding in the blink of an eye. A wave of white lab coats and slide rules streamed from the military installation into the Observatory Dome to witness the event. OoPjf-137d had traveled in the wormhole back by two days on a mission to find out how this undetected rogue asteroid got loose.

OoPjf-137d wanted to impress upon these scientists the urgency of the catastrophe to come in two days. The alien climbed the steep outer wall of the observatory and straddled the lens of the telescope, so that his body was magnified five hundred-fold for the scientists to see. They were astounded and spellbound at the spectacle.

"I must know," screeched OoPjf-137d in a terrifyingly strident staccato. "Are you developing a method to sling-shot asteroids in order to hit targets in space?" Following the command of the senior scientist, not a voice was raised. "Please do not be frightened," extolled the alien whose voice had gone beyond shrill and nasty. "I am here to warn you. It is too dangerous." No white lab coat broke the silence, but OoPjf-137d had an idea, based upon his cultural studies of humans.

"Let me shake your hand to prove my good intentions." The alien believed that a gesture of trust might help. The chief scientist extended his hand sheepishly, upon which OoPjf-137d wound a tendril firmly. The scientist, suddenly bug-eyed, saw a flash of light and then a stark scene from the surface of Quintila b unfolded. Many creatures like OoPjf-137d were climbing steep mountains in the Habitable Zone.

While the scientist was mesmerized, OoPjf-137d saw otherwise, and eves-dropped on the chief scientist's inner thoughts, hearing, "The Institute has been tracking the alien's trajectory for the past twelve days and is not convinced of this strange creature's benign intentions. In fact, we consider the alien a threat to earthlings. The alien is probably colluding with another space race to attack our planet by moving troops and weaponry through the wormhole while we are in disarray."

The chief winked at the other scientists, hinting that, "This would be a perfect time to test out our project and deflect a rogue asteroid to destroy the creature's wormhole." Shocked, OoPjf-137d heard his thoughts loud and clear.

OoPjf-137d pulled his tendril away abruptly, realizing that these earthling scientists were the culprits who would redirect a rogue asteroid to hit his wormhole, on August 1, but would miss their target and hit the northern waterway. He intuited that the settlement would take the impact of the impending tsunami, so as to save the scientists. OoPjf-137d bolted back to the wormhole and reset it for the next day, July 31st, so he could find and save the inhabitants before their dam would be sacrificed.

Eclipsing the setting sun over the vaulted spires of the settlement church on July 31st, the wormhole appeared as a blazing apparition. The townsfolk and their priestly entourage fell to their knees at the sight of the wormhole. OoPjf-137d, with tendrils in radiant, radial display on the steep precipice overlooking the settlement, implored, "Quick, join me. I am here to save you."

"My Lord, My Lord," rejoiced the priest. "We have been waiting an eternity for You to dwell among us." Each of the congregants grabbed onto a tendril, so that the Righteous could be hauled to the top of the craggy ridge to enter the wormhole. With all aboard, OoPjf-137d detonated the dam adjacent to the settlement, so that the consequential river surge into the abandoned settlement would provide a benign path to divert any future tsunami wave safely away from the Astronomical Institute. Oops redirected the wormhole forward in time by one day to notify Central Command.

Chapter Four

Flying out of the military installation at Central Command on August 1st, reconnaissance planes pursued their mission to destroy the settlement dam. To their amazement, the dam had already been shattered and the settlement flooded. They scoured the countryside for refugees, but none were to be found. The dam protecting the Astronomy Institute was intact, so they launched a rescue mission to evacuate the scientists.

All the members were transported safely. Once at Central Command, the chief scientist restated his encounter with the menacing alien two days earlier. Craig deployed his troops, just in case the alien, its wormhole, and perhaps an army of Quintilians should reappear again. Sited within moments, sure enough, the giant wormhole reappeared dark and frighteningly hostile in the afternoon sky. Craig assembled his infantry with artillery, stingers, and drones to intercept and destroy the spacecraft, should it be in attack mode.

Once stationed on the landing platform, the space module reassembled itself from the glittering droplets of cosmic debris that spewed from the core of the wormhole. Craig and his arsenal were poised to launch an attack, but as the hatch fizzed open, out poured the people of the settlement, waving their arms wildly and jumping exuberantly with gratitude and jubilation.

OoPjf-137d was the last to exit. Its tendrils grasped to find footing, but the creature lost its hold and tumbled down for a hard landing onto the tarmack and into a slimy pool of jet fuel and solid waste seepage from the water closet.

Meanwhile, the troops surrounded the embarrassed creature, preparing to take it into custody, when the people of the settlement locked arms together to shield the alien from harm. OoPjf-137d was immersed in an impenetrable bubble of love.

"Let's smoke him, General," implored the soldiers. "Over our dead bodies," the settlement people chanted defiantly. "He is our Lord Savior." Earnest knew that the fateful decision was his alone, and that his decision could alter the future and maybe even the past, and then the future again, and then maybe the past, again, possibly. Earnest reached out with his hand, and OoPjf-137d took a firm grip.

Epilogue

OoPjf-137d barely survived that desperate situation, some say by the fuzz of its tendrils. In fact, the alien did leave behind a few wisps of hairy spines coated with solid waste seepage, as a keepsake for future generations of earthlings to commemorate August 1st.

Under political pressure, Congress revised the H-1B visa program to limit telepathy without consent. As well, religious authorities of both worlds rededicated themselves to the project of bringing together the God of the Quintilians and the God of the Earthlings with new prayer communication protocols that might one day overcome the vexing disappointment of Divine Indifference.

But the real scientific revelation was that OoPjf-137d was actually a digitally constructed holographic AI avatar bot that escaped from an alien Quintilian civilization that went extinct long before the Earth was formed. Go figure.

The End

Abraham's Dilemma and Redemption

I

A thumping, melancholy heart burst within Abraham's chest, wrenching him awake from a fitful sleep. Something was not right.

From the silent campfire at the base of the holy altar, flickering patterns of muted light and shadow fluttered and danced through the billowing sheets of his desert tent, reached out to Abraham, imploring him to engage, to know.

The evil voices had returned. Distant mumbling spirits stalked him incessantly, skulking around and through the small crevasses of his mind. Indecipherable mutterings were everywhere. The hiss of the duplicitous snake, the menacing growl of the trickster coyote, the piercing howl of the moaning jackal lying in ambush, all murmured in his ears, like lurking intruders, observing Abraham from afar. *They are evil spirits*, thought Abraham, recalling the malevolent spirit gods of his father, Terah, who worshiped vindictive idols. Abraham was the wayward son, the rebel. The evil spirit gods were mindful of Abraham, too. They planted doubt and self-incrimination in his soul.

In desperate denial Abraham sprang to his feet and raced to his son's quarters. He turned over and over the bed sheets of his missing son, Ishmael. He dug frantically in the hope of holding him once more. The comforter that should have nurtured Ishmael lay as barren and empty as the grave of Sheol. Cascading tears etched long furrows down Abraham's weathered cheeks, like the deep ravines, where Ishmael likely took his last breaths, cursing his father in bewildered disappointment and rage for Abraham's unjustified and cruel estrangement, as Abraham's God inexplicably looked the other way.

Which of Terah's spirit idols would condone such a pitiful act? Yet was Abraham's act of estrangement and exile of Ishmael any different than his earthly father's banishment of Abraham to the godless desert to search for his true God? Surely, in an act of ironic retribution, Terah's vengeful spirit gods had taken Ismael, if only to revel in Abraham's hypocrisy. Vicious guilt was ever present, toying with Abraham, when the howls of the jackals would whisper incriminating thoughts of depravity and regret in his defenseless ears.

Abraham's dour introspection was interrupted by the whistling of distant desert winds, whipping up violently and flapping the fragile tent. Hoofs! The reverberating crescendo of rumbling hoofs shook the ground as they approached. They carried legions of marauding, vindictive spirit remains that had ruptured from the souls of Sodom's many dead, from whom was taken unjustly all they had in this life and all they would ever have to quench the thirst of Abraham's God for punishment. A jealous God, indeed, was Abraham's God, whose rigid embrace left Abraham mired in moral incoherence.

Descending upon his tent, the desert tumult swelled into a calamitous uproar! The angry desert rose up in judgment over Abraham and his God. Rumbling peels of angry thunder and mushrooming billows of swirling smoke and roiling ash engulfed Abraham's tent. Sharp razors of incensed sand and gravel stung Abraham's eyes and slashed his cheeks, rent open his garments, and cut his foreskin. Churning, irate vortices sucked up vengeful bones and skull fragments from the conflagration at Gomorrah and hurled them mercilessly at Abraham in retaliation. Fuming dust devils spun a web of anguish and cataclysm that engulfed Abraham's soul in shame and spiritual darkness. Abraham staggered and collapsed in despair, exhausted from his despondent grief. Protestation spent, the moral outrage of the shrieking gales lapsed into groveling moans. The growling howls of the jackals relented to a whimpering whisper, "Ishmael, Ishmael."

Abraham, the wounded soldier in defense of his God, revived to the pungently sweet fragrance of burning cedar, wafting from the smoldering campfire below his Lord's battered altar. Stubborn embers, still burning fiercely, launched passionate cinder and ash skyward, yearning for heaven, only to be arrested by the reverberant echoes of guilt and remorse. Charred, withered, crinkled cinder and ash drew downward, ever downward, to the cold earth. The spiritual chill of doubt and resentment that encrusted Abraham's soul had become so frozen and intransient that even the burning passion for his Lord's eternal flame could not thaw it.

Abraham's obedient ear turned. He heard the bellow of his Lord, commanding him to rekindle the luster of the battered altar. But, in truth, the luminescence of his God's eternal plan was dimming in Abraham's eyes, still obscured by images of pitiful Ishmael. His God, too, had His own doubts about Abraham's faith and commitment. What would Abraham's God require to assuage His doubts?

Lifting hopeful arms unfolded to the sky, Abraham inhaled the rapture of the immense and eternal nightly firmament, filled with glittering, celestial promises of a land to cultivate generations of his own progeny, who would praise and glorify his God, and, perhaps, grant Abraham absolution from his private shame and self-condemnation.

II

Sarah stood by the hearth, preparing breakfast, when Abraham trudged in and crumpled into his seat.

"Abraham," queried Sarah with a judgmental glare, "were you wandering last night, again, in the cold night air?" Abraham glumly stirred his soup, lifting clumps of cactus, scorpion, and toad, only to watch them drift lifelessly to the bottom of the bowl.

"This is all I have to work with, Abraham," chided Sarah. "It was better back home with your father, Terah. Do you remember? Lots of friends and family?"

An edgy silence grew between them. Abraham countered, "Our family is smaller now only because YOU threw out half of us!" Abraham saw Sarah ease into the silent shadows of the jackal's den.

Eyeing her wounded prey, Sarah growled with bared teeth, "That Arab, that slave, Haggar and her bastard son Ishmael were just temporary substitutes, until God brought us our true son, Isaac. They had no place here after Isaac was given to us by God, who promised us a home and a nation of families through our seed, the seed of Isaac, not that slave child, Ishmael, Abraham. We took our exile to find the true God, and we did, Abraham, you did! Your courage to break with the idol worshippers was a success. You should feel vindicated, re-assured, and validated."

"It was still cruel to exile them, Sarah. For all we know they died a miserable death in the desert," confided Abraham, hanging his limp body in supplication.

"This was the right thing to do," Sarah rebutted. "God sanctioned it. He said we may do with them what I want. God will see to everything. No need for self-indulgent sentimentality." Abraham shrugged, but not in agreement.

"Look, I will prepare for you your favorite treat, apple pudding," smiled Sarah, as she split the apples, saving the juicy exterior and tossing the undesirable and problematic core.

Sarah's crabapple trees seemed miraculously plump and abundant in her desert garden, thought Abraham to himself, *but in the barren desert they surely had shallow roots*. Abraham intuited that Sarah's moral façade was rooted in divisive jealousy, from which grew serpentine guile and indifference.

Abraham's contemplation took a darker turn. In his judgment, Sarah's wisdom hung like low fruit from the crabapple tree. Pity that her wisdom did not reach upward to the sanctity of the lives of others, like Ishmael and his slave mother, Haggar. The miracle of human life, of giving birth at so advanced an age as Sarah's, blinded her to the unspoken side of this gift. Sarah's moment of incredulous laughter belied her naivety, her blushing ignorance, that God would create life just for the two of them alone, without an ulterior motive. No declared quid pro quo. Here, from the dry, barren desert of his elderly wife sprung life. A miracle or mirage? A gift or an advance on a contract? Abraham shook his head to force out these troubling thoughts.

Abraham again awoke abruptly that night from a fitful sleep broken by the murmuring of the jackals. The campfire flickered with fluttering luminescent images. This time Abraham stared with new understanding. He could decipher a message, which could have come only from his God. Animal sacrifices were not sufficient to appease his petulant God, who was perturbed by Abraham's obstinate clinging to Ishmael. His God insisted that Abraham choose between human moral sentimentality and the Divine Plan. To shake Abraham to his core, God commanded Abraham to sacrifice Isaac. "Here I am," said Abraham, as would a servant to his master.

III

At dawn Abraham nudged Isaac to awaken him to what might be Isaac's last awakening. Abraham bundled wood chips and secretly packed a bag harboring the sacrificial knife. He commanded Isaac to accompany him and two servants to a distant location, Mount Moriah, to perform an animal sacrifice. Isaac, eager to please his father, joined enthusiastically. As the party left on their pack mules, Isaac asked Abraham why he did not bring a sacrificial sheep. "God will provide, God will provide" was Abraham's evasive mantra, using God's name in duplicitous conspiracy to deceive his son.

Arriving at the base of the holy mountain, Abraham and Isaac left the servants behind. They scaled the jagged rock formations overlying the darkly mysterious chasms secreted in the sacred mountain to reach the intended precipice overlooking the broad expanse of the Promised Land. The excited morning sky reddened with feverish anticipation. Isaac labored to carry the wooden stakes across his back and up the mount. As they approached the intended location, the sky yielded to darker hues, casting an ominous patina over the pair of ascending pilgrims.

Abraham commended Isaac to fold his arms over which Abraham twisted tight bindings. Puzzled, but compliant, Isaac knelt and then lay prostrate upon the rocky precipice, his wooly hair and sheepish eyes in obedient disbelief. Isaac's quizzical expression reached out to Abraham, but Abraham turned to grasp the sacrificial knife that he had hidden in the satchel. Abraham raised the knife above Isaac and to the heavens for God to see.

Abraham gazed over the Promised Land, preparing to lower the knife, but he hesitated, when he saw Isaac's face turn to abject terror. Resigned to God's commandment, Abraham's stalwart eyes shifted from Isaac to the heavens to await God's Word. The protesting howls of the jackals broke the ambivalent silence, as a gust of upstart wind swirled and spun a vortex of sand and dust.

From his inner chasm of regret, Abraham gazed down for one last look upon Isaac, his only remaining son, whom he loved and adored in equal measure to Ishmael. To his amazement, he no longer saw the face of Isaac. Instead, it was the face of his father, Terah, scowling with a judgmental glare trained on Abraham. Terah's face burst into laughter.

"Is this what you have come to, Abraham? All the way into the wilderness to give birth to a family of devotees to your God, and now you will kill your only remaining offspring, your only link to that legacy?" Chuckling. "Or maybe Isaac was just a fantasy to ease your doubts about some convoluted reason to sacrifice Ishmael to please your God. Is Isaac just a desert mirage or idol that you worshipped, and now will destroy, because God only loaned him to you to test your obedience?" Terah's voice howled and snarled over winds that tore into Abraham's psyche and seared his soul. "Go ahead, Abraham, kill your illusion of grandeur."

Abraham looked again to the silent heavens above for guidance. Frothy dust and debris, whipped up by impassioned winds, gusted from deep within the jagged edges of the rocky precipice, blinding his vision. He rubbed his eyes and gazed earthward to confront the face of his father, which, to his astonishment, morphed into the face of Sarah.

"Don't do it, Abraham," Sarah pleaded, her face contorted with grief and despair. "Do not condemn Isaac to the dank abyss of Sheol. He is all I have as my reward for abandoning my life among the benevolent spirits of my family in Ur." Her pleads burst into jackal wails of despondency.

Abraham, unmoved, gritty and determined to pass the test of his God's commandment, raised the knife to the heavens once again. Intrusive, ferocious surges of dust exploded from the demonic, now interior, whirlwinds of his soul, arresting as if toying with his wavering arm, emboldened, as the jackals mocked Abraham's indecision. He tried and failed once more to thrust the knife into the heart of Isaac.

To regain his determination, Abraham's weathered gaze refocused on the sacrificial target once more, but as his vision cleared, he no longer saw Isaac, or Terah or Sarah on the sacrificial altar. Abraham saw himself. It was Abraham, who lay prostrate, squirming and bound up like a naïve and confused victim in bondage to his own myopic, self-indulgent and humanly sentimental clinging to Ishmael.

Vision turned inward as Abraham went eyeball to eyeball with his God, unblinking and cleansed of human moral self-righteousness and sentimentality. In a flash of inner vision Abraham was struck by a jolting epiphany, as if awakening from his imaginary world of misplaced loyalty and emotional dissonance. Abraham now knew that the knife he raised against Isaac would ultimately kill only himself and his legacy, because the murder of his only remaining son with his own hands would condemn Abraham to a life of unremitting guilt and self-hatred, certainly not a spiritual frame of mind to found a nation devoted to a moral God.

What would be the consequence of my own spiritual suicide? thought Abraham. *If I die, so dies my God in the eyes of men and my generations to come*, reflected Abraham ironically. *Who will follow a murderer to pray at the holy altar?* For the first time Abraham had the inner vision to see his true bond with God, an epiphany for which he had always yearned.

Abraham's hardened knuckles thrust the knife downward with all his life's force, and plunged the blade into the heart of a wayward ram, stuck in the thicket nearby to which God drew Abraham's attention, after God got from Abraham the decision for which He'd hoped. Blood erupted, gushed, and sprayed upward toward the heavens, bloodying the skies with shards of bone and brain, which rained down on the dry desert like the withered, crinkled cinder and ash of the sacrificial fire. He turned to Isaac and cut his trappings, freeing both Isaac and Abraham from bondage. Abraham quickly threw the ram onto the sacrificial alter, so that the charred smoke would proclaim to the servants, Sarah and God, that the de facto sacrifice of Ishmael had been consummated. Abraham was free of guilt, resentment, and bondage to the shallowness of human codependency. Abraham embraced a higher calling to God's ultimate plan.

Epilogue

Abraham wafted billows of smoke skyward. He gazed with new vision and great relief upon Isaac and the serene expanse of his Promised Land. "This is mine for me and my progeny from Isaac's seed, in numbers more than the sands of the desert or the stars in the firmament. Over time into the infinite future my progeny will unite in a great chorus of praise to my legacy and my God, who has given this to me, and I to them, forever." Abraham repeated this to himself, until the sound of it rang true with a deafening, resounding echo that banished all memory of and attachment to Ishmael. The howl of the jackals was no more.

"Without me, my God would die in the eyes of men and my generations to come. God needs me as His partner." Quid pro quo.

Concluding the sacrificial offering, Abraham and Isaac packed up their belongings and descended the mountain to the waiting servants. Abraham and Isaac were quiet, for Abraham had nothing to say. They rarely spoke from that day forth.

That night Abraham awoke from a turbulent nightmare with visions of Ishmael's firstborn descendants in Egypt consumed by a divine scourge.

The End

About Ricky

(Inspired by actual events)

I

Ricky cringed as Emmet straight-arm slammed the heel of his palm flush against Arlo's cheek, aiming to rip Arlo's head clear off his friggin' neck. Arlo ricocheted off the panel of his prison cubicle, lunged at Emmet, and karate chopped him down viciously onto a pile of sweaty socks and jock straps. Emmet and Arlo were at it again.

"Whoa! Back off, guys!" bellowed a belching chorus of men from their nearby prison cubicles, each seated at his own office-styled desk with a computer screen, all the while laughing and pitching crumpled paper balls and airplanes at the ferocious combatants. "Ain't never no glory getting a whoppin' over this shit," mocked one of their fellow prisoners, dancing something like a video-simulated shadow box, while comically aping the two warriors. "Don't let this holographic fantasy football get your real skin in the game," chimed in another prisoner.

"Break it up, guys, and don't *alert the guards*!"

As predicted, prison guards in tight uniforms, lipstick, and female breasts descended on the quarrelling pair to enforce control and discipline. "You need to work out some tension, guys? Save it for the gym or the bar sector. For now, it's time out."

As defiant as all the other men, Emmet launched himself into the seat at the desk of his tiny prison cubicle, one hand grabbing the Coor's Light, the other fondling the joystick of his desk computer. To Emmet's delight the dark screen exploded with mesmerizing images of A-bomb blasts, colliding football helmets, crunching bones, blazing machine guns mowing down gargantuan monsters taunting fierce warriors with bulging, tattooed biceps and white knuckles clenched with the green blood and flesh of alien avatars.

From all sides surrounding Mike's prison cubicle, competing computer-simulated mayhem emanated from other paneled, office-styled partitioned prison cubicles, identical to Emmet's, in neat rows of adjacent cubicles, tens of thousands wide, forward and back, fading into the seemingly endless expanse of the Great Room. Perpetually lit up with intoxicating images of conflict and conquest, all living space in the Great Room was saturated with testosterone-laced bravado.

Then…entered Ricky, tippy toeing gingerly and unobtrusively on spindly legs around dirty dishes and spit balls at various stages of hardening on the littered floor. Ricky had wandered around the vast sweep of the Great Room for well-nigh all of his twenty years, wearing sports jerseys that he could never flesh out with manly muscles, and awkwardly intruding into manly talk with ill-timed growls and garishly pretentious gestures that the other men read as silly, even effeminate. His gangly gait and gentle sweeps of hair telegraphed a genteel nature, a refinement of attitude and intellect that men found perplexing, if not threatening. Failing to curry favor among the men, Ricky feigned a glistening smile, an obsequious posture, and dolefully desolate eyes that masked his unrelenting existential despair.

Ricky's survival strategy was to first skirt around the ruckus, then bumble his way back to his sector. Relieved to find his cubicle, but dismayed by the commotion, Ricky sought to commiserate with his cubicle neighbor, Bobby, but Bobby waved off Ricky's overtures. Bobby was laser focused on the holographic computer-simulated battlefield.

Bobby was a favorite among the prison guards: meek of temperament and forever fixated on his computer screen was the way the guards liked it. Absorbed in his PlayStation games for the entire day of every day, oblivious to the world around him, Bobby embraced the fantasy world, unlike Ricky, who just could not get into the games, nor find a suitable computer-generated avatar. All his sector buddies knew Ricky was an outlier, a misfit, who failed to progress through any scripted storyline.

Bobby, on the other hand, was acclaimed as one of the truly great manipulators of the computer games. All his knowledge, life's experience, fleetness of skill, foresight and steadiness of hand was invested since his childhood in reaching "end-game" to "unlock the hard-mode." From there he'd be transported to the next level, be it level six or ninety-six, or a seemingly infinite numbers of levels, forward and backward, spanning the endless horizon of gaming programs, littered with the discarded debris of forgotten computer simulations in revolving loops, forever returning to the next beginning, but only a beginning without an end. None of the prisoners ever escaped addiction to the holographic images that blurred the distinction between reality and simulation.

When Bobby peered into the mirror of his flat screen, reflected back he saw only the avatar of an ageless, rugged, chiseled-faced, scruffy behemoth with a broadly tattooed shoulder and a cigar stub dangling from his snarling lips, one hand blazing away on a machine gun and the other spraying grenades.

Ricky leaned in on Bobby, and watched while Bobby reached the critical moment in the encounter simulation and braced himself, for the ultimate confrontation had arrived. A galvanic force surged through his fingers to ignite his avatar for the final assault. He had enemy combatants under siege. A Martian warrior burst into view from the left, but Bobby adroitly vaporized him, showering shards of bloody score points onto the computer screen. Hordes of Hoary Huns streamed in from the right, but Bobby mowed them down to clear his path to the rendezvous point. Blaring sirens, Blackhawk helicopters, surging warriors, and gun duels leapt off his computer screen, as he craftily navigated the hostile combatants. Fixated with singular focus, he doggedly pursued the phantom images to complete his…

"Time for dinner!" twanged the intrusive kitchen guard, sporting a hairnet and apron. "Put down the joystick and clear your desks."

Yanked from his reverie, Bobby did not see the crouching gunmen coming for him, so in a blaze of crossfire, Bobby's avatar was blasted into smithereens. The blinking red light on his screen tolled that the game was over. "Damn it, I was so close!" wailed Bobby, flicking away the locks of hair that caressed his furrowed forehead. Bobby gave the guard a derisive sneer and an obscenely dismissive gesture. "Go away. I need to complete my mission, reach 'end game,' and 'unlock the hard mode' to soar to the next level, until there is nothing left to conquer."

"Later, Shogun," chided the guard. "Time to put it down for a while and eat your dinner."

Meanwhile, as was his habit, Ricky slumped vacuously into his seat in Great Room cubicle #10,509. The three barren office panels of his tiny prison cubicle surrounding him stared down at Ricky resolutely, subduing and restraining him. With vision blocked from three sides, Ricky reflected morosely into the past behind him, into the recollections of his youth.

One of his earliest memories, before arriving in the Great Room, was pacing about the playpen. Other boys were likewise pacing restlessly, taking a break from their superhero avatars to push or shove each other, or stare comatose at the TV screen. Little girls would buzz in and out of the free zone that encircled the playpen. They were on their way to dance lessons and instructional classes that their mothers would arrange. Strangely, Ricky did not recall his father. Neither did any of the men in the Great Room.

II

One day the guards escorted in a visitor, a Trina Manfred Hollings. Ricky's cubicle was situated near the perimeter door of the Great Room, so that from his perch he could see who was coming and going. Trina was chubby and her demeanor whiny, but her darting eyes, searching.

"Here to make a selection?"

"Yes," acknowledged Trina with a sultry wink. "I want a gentleman just for the night."

"Very well, Ms. Manfred Hollings," consented the guards, and advised, "May we suggest Sergio? He seems 'ripe,' if you know what we mean." Giggles flittered about.

Ricky reacted. The very idea of non-consensual sex with this woman was nauseatingly repugnant to Ricky's proclivities. His confinement in the Great Room was making him just as sick, but not sick enough to get him out. He was trapped, just like all the other men.

By great fortune Ricky identified another door, rarely used, near the perimeter entrance. It connected to the nurse's station. Ricky felt some odd fascination with the nursing station. Then, from a jolt in his imagination exploded an epiphany.

It turned out earlier that day Ricky was sampling a new video game recommended by Bobby. This one featured an unusual transgender character. Ricky was intrigued by this and wondered what it would be like to take on a transgender avatar. From this, Ricky hatched a plot to escape, figuring that an attractive transgender character could ALSO be the ticket out of his predicament. "A two-for-one deal," Ricky chortled. He waited for the inevitable flaring of tempers. So, when the guards were subduing the bad boys, Ricky made for the nurse's station.

"Were you hurt?" queried the nurse.

"Yes, I have been hurting for as long as I can remember. You see, there was a big mistake made long ago," pleaded Ricky. "I was born into the body of a man, but in my heart and soul, I am a woman."

"Oh, my poor dear," exclaimed the nurse, "why didn't you tell us this when you were a child? We could have saved you so much pain. Nevertheless, it's never too late to make the change." The nurse gave Ricky his first shot of estrogen.

Over the next few weeks Ricky observed a dramatic reconfiguration. His beard vanished, and his facial features softened. His hips rounded, and his voice floated into the soprano range. Ricky approved of his new avatar, and even enjoyed applying lipstick. Ricky mused, "Perhaps just a slight elevation of my cheek bones with blusher, and a rounding of my eyes to create a look of compassion and acceptance with maybe just a hint of subterranean intensity," said Ricky, reddening her lips, while giggling and flittering her eyelashes.

It was not long before Ricky mirrored the semblance of a real-to-life woman. "Remarkable," gloated the nurse, admiring Ricky's transformation. "Now it is time for the ultimate step, and proceed onto castration."

This was one step more than Ricky wanted, so she needed to act fast. Stealthily, while the nurse left the office to get the surgical equipment, Ricky sauntered with grace and aplomb between the distracted guards. The last thing the Great Room saw of Ricky was the backside of her billowing pastel shirt and two thin hairless legs skipping girl-ishly from the bouncing butt end of her cute blue jeans.

Soon, Ricky encountered a gaggle of women at their worksta-tions. One of the women was data imputing with one hand and cra-dling her breastfeeding infant with the other arm, all the while zooming virtually on her iPhone headset. Her compatriots were also feverishly multitasking. Above the hum of continuous small talk, one woman erupted, "These tasks are overwhelming! If I don't get it done right, I will have let everyone down. I can't bear the thought of being a fucking failure in the eyes of all my friends. What would they say?" Another woman cried out, "I'm having a panic attack. Where are we going with this?"

Ricky placed a warm and reassuring hand on the shoulder of the first woman, saying, "Don't worry. The real beauty in life is being true to yourself." The woman looked up at Ricky's reassuring manner and accepting eyes. Ricky continued, "Your intensity and commitment to your friends and family will be your reward and satisfaction. We all go through it together."

The gaggle calmed down amidst a growing connection and en-veloping atmosphere of peace and camaraderie. "Let's do a group hug," and Ricky extended her arms to swaddle the women in a swath of self-acceptance. There ensued a palpable and marvelous release of tensions, as the spirit of sharing and community wiped away all the troubling thoughts and worries.

Among the group was an older, stately woman who approached Ricky. "Hi, I am the mayor of Matriarchville. I am so glad that you came through for our group. We should do lunch together."

On the following day, Ricky ascended to the tenth floor of the mayoral building. The mayor warmly welcomed Ricky into the ante-chamber. Ricky was impressed by all the memorabilia commemorat-ing the ascendency of women to the highest levels of power.

"It was a tough climb," explained the mayor, "but the results were worth it. *No more wars, abrasive individualism, and social discord.*

We finally have a tranquil world at peace with goodness, shared equally by all."

Ricky gazed at the Scales of Justice in the mayor's memorabilia curio, and acknowledged that women were equal to men, but were they any better? Ricky was hoping that women had something better to offer men.

"But what about the men?" blurted Ricky, surprised by her uncharacteristic assertiveness.

"I'm surprised you ask," replied the mayor with invective femininity. "I would have thought your upbringing would have taught you how we deal with men. They are housed in Great Rooms, to monitor them, channel them, and control their noxious impulses. 'XX.' Okay, but why the 'Y,' right?" The mayor leaned toward Ricky. "Let me explain. Men are genetically defective, an evolutionary vestige of a primitive era in human history. Like any vestigial organ of the body politic, men can be no more than a plague and source of societal dysfunction. For their own sake, they need to be isolated and contained."

"But then, if all men are criminalized, aren't Great Rooms just like prisons?" contended Ricky, straining to veil her unchecked rebellious glare through slits of heavy mascara.

"These men are prisoners of their own malevolent constitutions and incorrigible flaws. All toxic swagger, but weak and frail, is what they're made of. All have inherited the scourge of misogamy. We are all much safer with men in Great Rooms."

"But what happens if the room has an emergency…like a fire?"

The mayor gestured to the glass ceiling above, through which was situated a steady red light, which emitted from a small switchbox, the "Nexus" release button. "In a crisis the Nexus switch will open the doors to all the Great Rooms and release the men inside."

Ricky stared forlornly through the glass ceiling and wondered whether one day someone might break the glass and throw the switch.

III

Ricky was well liked among all her new friends. They trusted her, as one of their own. Ricky became quite adept at pleating cloth napkins. Her flowing pastel shirts and French fingernails impressed everyone with her gentility. The ebb and flow of her sociable chat over Mah-Jongg sprung effortlessly without reflective filter.

Unfortunately, as time went on, the physical effects of the estrogen treatments began to wear off. Her voice would crack and quack, as if going through puberty. A subtle five o'clock shadow made a cameo appearance. Her mind might become impatient and drift away from endless loops of inconsequential banter. The voice in her head once again sounded male.

Others soon took note. "Ricky, you're looking a little mannish lately. Are you all right? Do you need to see a doctor?" On the inevitable day, Ricky was evil eyed by a woman who was speaking vociferously with some guards, periodically gesturing at Ricky from a distance. The guards gazed on with a scowl. Ricky knew his camouflage was blown, and he could no longer hide behind the facade he'd cultivated to win acceptance. Apologies would appear hollow and contrived. Once caught and his true gender revealed, he would be slammed back into his prison cubicle in the Great Room, forever.

Feet! Ricky heard the stamping of feet, many feet, ever louder, coming for him from behind. The childhood urge to run and hide kindled his hairy legs in reflex preparation for flight. Yet, he stood his ground, as a sudden awakening, another epiphany, calmed his restless pacing and transported Ricky into deep soliloquy.

"Hath not a man eyes?" waxed Ricky, "Yes, cursed to wander and deceive, but also blessed to envision language of the deepest compassion and insight, like Shakespeare. Hath not a man hands? Yes, cursed to manipulate, violate, and crush, but also to transform spirituality beyond imagination, like Michelangelo. Hath not a man 'mind'? Yes, cursed to yield to cruelty and malice, but also blessed to shepherd human destiny into the farthest reaches of divine providence, like Einstein." A surge of testosterone ignited galvanic forces within Ricky's core, electrifying and transforming him to pursue his new mission *NOW.*

Ricky eluded the security guards and took the elevator to the mayor's office, where one guard confronted him from the right. Ricky grabbed her taser to stop her in her tracks. The next guard, approaching from the left, put up a better fight, but Ricky grabbed her weapon and neutralized her, showering shards of bloody score points onto the video screen in the reception room. The mayor herself jumped him from behind, but Ricky threw her to the carpet. Waves of Warring Women poured out of the elevator, coming for him. He slam-bolted the entrance door, scaled the tall ladder, and drove a hammer, smashing the glass ceiling above. Guards were pounding the entrance to the mayor's suite. Blackhawk helicopters buzzed the building. Explosions rumbled in the distance. Ricky ripped open the cover of the Nexus box, just as a rush of women crashed through the door. He activated the switch, confirmed the blinking red light, and ran for the balcony.

From his perch on the ledge of the tenth floor, Ricky witnessed beams of helicopter lights scouring the tsunami of men who streamed out from the Great Room, flooding the streets below. Sirens screeched. Helicopters filled the air with torrents of wind and debris. The door to the antechamber burst open. Guards crashed through the room, coming for Ricky. For the first time in his life Ricky felt a deep sense of existential purpose and gratification. Contentedly, he closed his eyes....

Epilogue

"Hey, dude…wake up." Bobby stood over Ricky, while sporting a grin of admiration. Ricky raised his heavy head and scratched at his two-day-old beard stubble.

"Congrats, man. So, you finally found a video game to your liking. I knew you would dig this one, buddy. AND YOU DID IT! You completed your mission, freeing all the prisoners. Dude, I could not have done it better myself," he proclaimed, and confided with a wink. "Quite a sexy avatar, I might add…. Ready for the next level?"

With bleary eyes Ricky scanned the dreary panels of prison cubicle #10,509. His computer screen flashed a blinking red light. Ricky's ear inched closer to the screen to hear the deeply monotone computer voice announcing, "You have reached 'end game.' 'Hard mode' is now unlocked."

The End

The Grandfather Clock

Elevated on the tips of her tiny toes, Rachel's probing eyes could barely peer over the window's ledge to survey the gloomy streets below. Immersed in darkness, a lonely lamplight cast a cone of illumination over animated men searching for Jews. With rifles hoisted over their shoulders, the men boldly displayed swastikas on their military hats and jackets.

Rachel's mother, Chaika, broke the silence with an urgent message. "Come away from the window, Rachel, so they don't see you. We don't want to attract their attention." Her mother beckoned by the wave of her hand to join her at the Shabbos table in the shadows at the center of the living room.

Rachel, squinting, hand-walked her way through the darkened apartment, inching around the aged, deep-buttoned Chesterfield, and creeping over the musty Persian throw rug, muted in deep purples and green. For guidance, she ran her fingertips along the faded wallpaper in floral design, selected by her parents for its rhythmic balance, order, and harmony. Photographs of family, framed in tasteful display, clung to the wallpaper for support. As she edged across the drafty fireplace, her saddened gaze ascended along the tall, hand-engraved, mahogany box, positioned as a majestic sentinel, upon which was perched the face of the silent grandfather clock, seeming to oversee Shabbos from above.

"Come help me light the candles to welcome in the Sabbath," implored Menachem, who gently spread over his shoulders his lovingly adorned tallit, which displayed bright biblical scenes of ancient Jewish worship. He stroked the thick waves of his greying beard and adjusted his yarmulke over his smooth head. Curls of dangling hair strands cascaded over both ears.

"We must fulfill our part of the Covenant to worship God, so God will hear us, and take good care of us," explained her father. In Rachel's imagination, the austere face of her grandfather was engraved in the wooden casing of the clock face, which seemed to approve with a loving nod.

To begin the service, her mother, cloaked in a dark, modest dress, laid the embroidered cloth over the challah. She ignited the candles that accompanied the ritual wine glasses on the sacred table. Chanting softly, she first closed then covered her eyes with the cup of her palms, momentarily hiding from view the family's dire circumstances. Her father chanted softly into God's ear so as to not be heard by soldiers in the street, and likely those in their building, as well.

Rachel's father spoke. "Barukh ata adonai Eloheinu. Blessed art thou, oh Lord our God, who is trustworthy in His covenant to fulfill His sacred promise to shield and protect His people, Israel. With a mighty hand God will rescue the people of Israel from their travails, as is our Lord's solemn promised never to forsake His people, when they were enslaved in Egypt."

Watch over us, thought Rachel, who then studied the face of the silent grandfather's clock, hugging the fireplace mantle. The hands of the clock, pointing up at ten and two, appeared to her like her father's arms unfolded and reaching to the heavens in prayer.

"I wish Grandfather could be with us tonight," whispered Rachel, interrupting the prayers.

Chaika explained with gentle directness, "Grandfather Yitzhak's clock stopped ticking on the day he was taken by the soldiers, as if the clock knew that grandfather had passed in their hands. Our deepest wish is for this lovely clock to welcome grandfather's spirit to return and live quietly among us always."

Her mother was about to remove the linen covering the challah, when loud knocking reverberated through the door and throughout the apartment.

"Achtung!" bellowed the soldier's voice. "Wer ist da?" Recognizing the impending peril, Rachel and her parents scrambled for cover.

"Mach sofort die fur auf!" Within the moment, two husky SS officers crashed the door open with a mighty fist, and surveyed the apartment lit only by two Shabbos candles.

"Sind Sie auch Judisch? Hander hoch. Juden verboten und infiziert ungeziefer!" Rachel's parents scurried behind the pantry curtain, dragging Rachel in tow.

"Rachel," Chaika insisted. "Hitler told the soldiers that Jews were vermin to be exterminated. Our lives are in danger should the soldiers find us. So, hush!"

I will pray for grandfather's protection, thought Rachel.

The thunderous rumble of a passing tank shook violently the apartment building to its foundation. With that, the grandfather clock revived to "bong, bong"; then commenced to "tick, tock, tick, tock." Rachel's eyes shown radiantly. She turned in amazement to her parents. "Momma, Momma," Rachel spoke above a whisper. "I hear it. Tick, tock, tick, tock. The clock is saying 'Yitzhak, Yitzhak.' Do you hear it?" Rachel's voice now rose in volume. "Grandfather is reaching out to us. I must go to the clock for his protection."

"Quiet, Rachel," implored Chaika. "We must remain silent and not attract the soldiers."

"No. Momma," Rachel pleaded. "The grandfather clock is calling to us. He wants me to go to him." Rachel loosened her mother's grip and clambered on all fours through the apartment, reaching out fearlessly to the voice of her grandfather.

The heads of the soldiers turned to the muffled rumble of Rachel scurrying across the Persian rug to reach the loudly animated grandfather clock. Catching a fleeting glimpse of her, one of the soldiers shouted, "Wer da? Handenen hoch." After a moment of silence, the soldiers let loose a blinding hail of bullets that tore through the sofa, releasing feathers and fragments of wood chips into a cloud of gunfire smoke. The butt end of their rifles slashed across the sacred table, smashing the Kiddush glasses and spewing the red wine like blood onto the Persian rug.

Chaika and Menachem huddled silently, praying that Rachel would emerge from the darkness. Yet she was silent, even after the soldiers left. The ticking of the grandfather clock had also gone silent. Rachel's breathless parents stared silently into the darkness of their apartment.

Gazing from the broken Shabbos candles and across the silent apartment and through the window looking outward and downward, they saw the gloomy street below was silent. All the streets of the city were silent. The countryside extending from the city to the sea was silent.

All the earth was silent. All the celestial candles, as stars in the sky and a trillion galaxies beyond, as far as all humanity knew, were silent. The entire universe in its totality from the beginning of time remained silent.

The End

The Wishing Wall

Bullied birds, tumbling and twirling in turbulent torrents of hot desert wind, repelled off the massive, bone-dry blocks of ancient stone, from which was forged the Western Wall of Jerusalem's eternally sacred Temple. Little Rachel's innocent gaze ascended upward, wishing to grasp the wall's profundity, tame its unspeakable power, and scale its boundless heights in a single, ephemeral glance. No doubt displeased by this impudently cursory treatment, the inscrutably taciturn monolith leaned with the full force of its formidable, earthly gravitas to repel Rachel backwards, awestruck, into her mother's arms.

With reassurance from mother's steady hand, Rachel drew from her purse pocket a blank paper note, upon which she was to inscribe her prayers, and then insert the note respectfully into the wall's austere bulwark, as was tradition. Rachel termed it fancifully the "Wishing Wall," expressing a child's vision of what others termed the "Wailing Wall," an axis mundi for plaintiffs humbly praying for Divine Salvation.

While Rachel was writing her thoughts, the paper escaped from her hand, flapping on the wings of a great gust of wind. The partially inscribed page came to rest in the hands of a nearby woman, whose elderly face was etched by tears, that carved long furrows down her weathered cheeks, like the deep, desert ravines, where her sons likely took their last breaths during the war. As the woman began to write her prayer on Rachel's paper, another surge of wind flicked from her hands the unfinished note and delivered it to a man seated in a wheelchair next to her. Paralyzed in his right arm, he began scribbling with his shaky left hand, but, again, a mischievous ghostly courier swept it from him and carried it to a young woman, his caretaker, whose round, pregnant belly looked to Rachel as big as the whole world.

And so it went. The paper flew light as a feather, tumbling from one to the next. From a priest to a rabbi to a monk, to a single mother with a handicapped child, to a refugee in tattered clothes, to a business man searching for a moral compass, to a politician repentant in shame, to a physician overwhelmed with responsibility, to an addict without recourse, to a pessimist wallowing in despair, to a man consumed with anger, and then back to Rachel's gentle but firm grasp, thus completing the circle of pilgrims who surrounded her in silent despair and supplication.

Rachel scribbled her name at the very bottom of the crowded page, folded it, and searched for a crack in the wall's defenses. The excited late afternoon sky reddened with feverish anticipation, as the silent assembly of hopeful pilgrims searched for a sign of God's good graces. As if to signal that the promise of divine restoration and blessing was at hand, the early evening sky yielded to cooler, violet hues, casting a soothing patina of judgment, hope, and reconciliation over the assembly, as the turbulent gusts abated, and the battered birds once again sailed in gentle curls and kindred formations.

The End

Room with a View

The police were forced to break down the door to room 304 after tenants, as high up as the fifth floor, complained about the stench. The apartment was devoid of furniture, save for a single straight-backed wooden chair cradling a corpse, which faced the window overlooking the decimated nuclear facility across town. The plant had been bombed a week prior by a yet undeclared terrorist group. "Apparently an inside job," announced the FBI.

The corpse sat upright, restrained by duct tape. Decomposition had already sheered rotting flesh off its face. Even more grotesque were its blown-out eye sockets. Preliminary forensics estimated that the eyes had been sucked out after the terrorist attack, implying that the corpse had been positioned to witness the attack before its death. Investigators wondered if the corpse might belong to the Minister of National Security, Eric Stryker, who had vanished days before the bombing incident.

"We absolutely need to do brain surgery immediately," said the forensic surgeon, while loading the corpse onto the ambulance.

"Excuse me, Doctor," protested the Chief of Police, grabbing the scalpel from the doctor's hand. "He's dead. Surgery will only tamper with evidence."

Irritated, the surgeon lectured, "If we act quickly, we can remove from his temporal lobe those neurologic circuits that imprinted memories of the hours before the victim's death. Then we can integrate the encoded circuitry imprints into a neuro-cellular matrix, from which our biological 3D printer can generate a flash drive."

Melanie stepped in assertively to support the forensic doctor's claim. "Downloads of the flash drive will allow us to collect visual evidence directly from the minister's brain circuits, perhaps right up to the moment of his assassination," she explained. Melanie was the forensic team coordinator, who took charge of all evidential protocols.

Once back at headquarters Melanie pivoted to assign duties to her team of forensic experts with an air of confidence that far exceeded her age of thirty-two. She had been hand-picked by the Minister of National Security as the most competent for the job, "over a pack of competing misogynist hyenas," in Melanie's opinion. Eric considered her his next in line because he recognized in her approach an innovative vision for an integrated forensic team with a diversity of expertise.

This brings us to Rufus.

Melanie selected Rufus as the cornerstone of her forensic team, over the objections of her superiors, who considered the twenty-ish Rufus a hapless waif, who levitated cluelessly down a digital yellow brick road in some enchanted cyberland. Melanie, on the other hand, recognized in Rufus a unique mix of super-nerd wizard and sweetheart. They immediately bonded to each other, like Dorothy and the Scarecrow in a land of forensic cyber-crime.

Melanie turned to Rufus, who, at that moment, was totally absorbed in bouncing a rubber ball off the tiled cubicle walls of the conference room in and around piles of blinking computers stacked as high as skyscrapers.

"Rufus!" insisted Melanie, catching the rubber ball in midair. "You need to focus." As if in a cyber trance, Rufus's head, ablaze in a fiery red mohawk, rotated toward Melanie like R2D2 with doe-eyes. He frumped his expansive butt into the chair of his computer desk, shoved in the flash drive, pounded his forehead so as to force out any remaining alternative realities, and conjured up some techy magic.

The computer-generated images downloaded off the flash drive showed that the corpse was seeing both the intact nuclear facility through the window AND the reflected image of the victim's face in the window glass. Facial recognition programs confirmed that the reflected face was in fact that of the Minister of National Security himself, Eric Stryker.

Melanie's jaw went slack, so shocked and devastated was she at the discovery of the minister's presence in the apartment staged by the terrorists, and, worst of all, witnessing his grisly death at their hands. Her fingers quivered over the keyboard controls.

Eric had been the leader of the forensic team with Melanie's assistance as its longstanding liaison to the National Security apparatus. Melanie prided herself as a good judge of character, and she had more than great admiration for Eric's manner in matters of authority. She respected his fairness and openness, but more so his gentile and warm style. Over time they had moved from a professional collegial relationship to a closer, more personal, and affectionate vibe. She just could not believe that Eric would have misled her so thoroughly for the sake of subterfuge. "It just wasn't like him," whispered Melanie through her quivering lips.

A buzz of chatter swirled around the computer room and through the forensic team. "What was the minister doing in there?" one agent asked.

"Looks like he was in on it, just like the FBI said," intimated another with snide clicks of his tongue.

Melanie resented the denigrating suspicions voiced among her colleagues implying that the minister was somehow connected to the plot to destroy a government facility, much less to coordinate with international terrorists. Latent office tensions bubbled to the surface, setting up cross currents of heated debate and insinuations. Exasperated, Melanie bolted for the bathroom, while, on cue, into the conference room stepped Barker, the Undersecretary of Homeland Security. The effect of Barker's presence on the forensic team was palpable.

Few would have not considered Julius Barker the apparition of a haughty vulture. The broad sweep of his winged shoulders gave ascension to a narrow head and jutting chin, that projected forward well below the level of his collarbone. His scythe-like nose pivoted side-to-side when surveying each member of the team, looking for dead-beat meat, as would a bird of prey. He always made an effort to appear pleasant, but today his forced veneer was erased quickly by the twitching of his lips, like talons, sensing a kill going down.

Meanwhile, Melanie's shoes clacked around the bathroom tile before she abruptly stopped. With a deep sigh she dialed up the reception desk at Island Vacation Agency. Melanie's heard her own broken voice stutter into her cell phone to cancel her reservation. Without Eric, their Pacific Island plans lay in ruin. She took a good long look into the mirror.

Was it all just a ruse to set her up as a loyal but hapless team leader? The sympathetic mirror said that her mascara was smeared from tears. Her wavy blond hair was shorter now than it was ten years ago, when she first met Eric. Her cobalt blue eyes sparkled when she visualized Eric caressing her shoulder and wide-eyed exploration of her dimpled face and supple body. Melanie's saddened eyes searched the mirror for reassuring answers.

Then the mirror spoke back to her harshly. "*Look at me,*" shouted the face, the angry face staring straight back at her. "*Reality check, girl. Whatever the outcome, you'll deal with it later. Now get back to work!*"

Melanie waited a moment for her fuming anger to evaporate before she rejoined the forensics team, busy wrestling with possible strategies to examine the nuclear plant for clues. Direct inspection was prohibited due to leaked radiation debris scorching the plant's perimeter. Perhaps the assassination room had clues, but the reconstituted memory banks from the Minister's brain had unfortunately bccn partially degraded post-mortem, frustrating attempts to identify other faces in the room. Nonetheless, uncovering all events prior to the explosion in the reactor were now a priority and goal of forensic analysis under Melanie's direction. Consequently, how to access and analyze this elusive data was the issue. Alternative proposals were debated.

Amid the ruckus Rufus up and bumbled to his feet to propose a novel approach in his usual techy, convoluted manner of nerd-speak. "Listen up, team buddies," Rufus proclaimed. "I have a sure-fire plan to upload the captured fragments of memory in the minister's flash drive into a holographic recreation of the minister's brain, thus constituting a chimeric avatar/hybrid species, storable in the cyber-Cloud."

(No small matter, this avatar technology was actually invented by Rufus. He and his techy friends had already been using a program for some time that permitted the insertion of specific memories into experimental generic avatar brains floating in the cyber-cloud.)

Rufus blabbered on, "The holographic hybrid could commingle ongoing memories of the avatar brain with those recently captured memories on the flash drive. If this plan works, we might retrieve more memories from the minister's brain prior to his death. New evidence arising from the fusion of both ongoing and embedded memory circuits could be downloaded from the Cloud and witnessed directly by the team in real time. Got it?"

The forensic experts shook their heads in dumbfounded silence and mumbled incoherently among themselves. "So, then what?" one asked politely.

"Don't worry, team buddies," reassured Rufus, flapping his wrists in a fit of frolicking enthusiasm. "Once the holographic avatar/hybrid brain and memory flash drive have been reconstituted in the Cloud, we can guide it into the minister's pre-death brain by a recent innovation in time travel, which I'll set for about a week ago."

The team watched Rufus set to work repurposing the minister's hybrid avatar brain to serve as a template for time teleportation by way of the Toggle Retrograde Time Travel Transmitter System (TRTTTS). This top-secret experimental protocol, developed by NASA scientists, was designed to insert the mental states of an avatar brain into deep-time intersection points that momentarily appear within the frothy quantum matrix of space-time. This model worked well within the normal time zones on Earth, so the avatar could function up to twenty-four hours prior to recording time, but had not been tested for multiple time zones over the course of days to weeks.

Nonetheless, Rufus's persona of bubbling optimism infected the team. "Once inserted, the avatar complex could be guided to an intended recipient in a selected time zone, in this case that of the minister's brain as it functioned a week ago."

"Great, but how do we guide the avatar/hybrid through space/time to its intended target?" questioned one of the team members. Rufus informed the group that at the time Eric Stryker was sworn into office, he agreed to have embedded in his brain a homing chip connecting his mind to the Toggle system, preserved, and memorialized in the Cloud. By homing in on the targeted device, the implanted avatar hybrid brain could transmit the minister's thoughts, as far back in time as a week prior to his death. The prospect of gathering new clues and, as a bonus, perhaps additional memories that identify suspicious actors within the minister's inner circle during the critical interval, jacked up the team's resolve.

In fact, their efforts paid off. Retro-time insertion of the avatar hybrid into the mindset of the minister a week prior to his death generated images for the team to analyze. Melanie was most impressed. *Imagine if I could enter Eric's mind*, pondered Melanie in the quiet recesses of her private thoughts. *Was he ever thinking of me, the way I thought of him?*

The first images of the minister's thoughts unfortunately blurred facial features. Rufus attributed this data obscuration to resistance by the minister's hybrid brain to accept the retrograde microprogramming of the disturbing murder images recorded at the time of his death.

"Eric's having difficulty self-identifying with the memories of his future self that foreshadow his impending murder," opined Rufus. "So, let's try hypnosis."

With his trademark unrestrained enthusiasm Rufus comically gyrated and mimed a sorcerer with big arms waving in squares and ellipses, which did nothing to endear him to the more serious members of the team. Responding to the communal pressure of disapproving eyes, Rufus sank back into his laptop, tapped feverishly on the keys, and initiated a second upload.

Why hypnosis? Rufus and his techy ilk had studied hypnotic techniques to enhance the "Power of Suggestion." After years of analysis of propaganda techniques Rufus mastered the subtle art of psychological persuasion. "Did you know," said Rufus, "clever ad execs, politicized mass media, and TV ads, targeting lonely placebo seekers, crafted ways of achieving tacit complicity with propaganda messaging into the mesmerized minds of viewers with psychological tricks of denial of cognitive dissonance, motivated delusions, and rationalized derangement syndromes?" Melanie suspected that Rufus had given himself over completely to the black arts of mind control, not for self-seeking, personal advantage over others, social status, or the vanity of power, but rather as homage to the forces of the unconscious Mind.

"Wanna bet that hypnosis could overcome the minister's resistance?" repeated Rufus. Sure enough, a second upload seduced the minister's avatar/hybrid into a powerful trance-like state, compelling him to accept all memory messaging, however alarming. With rhythmic pulses of suggestible commands, the minister began to self-identify freely with his future memory fragments. Finally, the Toggle Thought Transporter device relayed back genuine, uninhibited mental impulses of the minister's ongoing experiences and thoughts from the Cloud. A flood of memory segments poured forth from the transporter devise, so that Melanie and her team could reconstruct the minister's life from memories.

Eyeing the first memory troves fed forward, the forensic team was surprised to witness the first scene opening with the minister presiding over a private, unscheduled meeting with a small group of, as yet, unidentified individuals, roughly a week prior to his death. The minister was easy to identify, due to his lanky physique, long, ruddy face, and cropped red hair, resembling the head of a kitchen match, earning him the surname/nickname "Striker." The minister was striding forcefully side-to-side at the head of the group and waving his arms in pleading gesture. A scruffy man with a mangy beard and facial tattoos jumped to his feet, shouting, "Why should we wait?"

Facial recognition profiling identified some of the attendees as known enemy combatants, terrorist operatives from Syrian and Ethiopian conflicts, last seen in the Ukraine. Other critical faces remained obscure due to partial degradation of post-mortem memory circuits.

Rufus set to fine tuning the images when the feed suddenly went blank. Just then, Richard Barker strode into the room along with several of his cronies. "Oh, oh," signaled Rufus. "Here comes Mr. Silverback."

Barker took an imposing power stance with fists dug into his hips and sharply contoured elbows projected outward from his grey suit, like wings of a vulture. He declared, "Okay. Listen up! I'm now the acting Minister of National Security in place of the deceased AND disgraced, Eric Stryker." Silence blew through the team council room, as the undersecretary's targeted gaze strafed each team members for signs of mutiny. Paralyzed members of the team sitting along the table's edge stared back at Barker with blank, plastic eyes like ducks in a carnival shooting gallery.

Melanie alone squirmed, gnashed her teeth, bit down on her pencil harder than usual, and finally flung the gnawed pencil across the room. Her hardened nail polish tapped impatient staccatos on her desktop. In her opinion *Barker was a politically talented but tainted climber in the national security apparatus. Worse, he was of the seedy type, who wanted to rule, but knew not how to serve. He was corrupt enough to use his position and proclivity for dominance to master others for personal advancement.*

Melanie had a deep distrust of Barker. He disrespected Eric, dismissing him as an incompetent subordinate. Barker caught a glance of Melanie, who gazed askance assiduously from him and his entourage.

"Melanie," commanded the testy undersecretary. "You are to turn over immediately all your downloaded feeds to me and my personal team of investigators, before you inspect any of them yourself. I am the only official here with adequate security clearance to review them. Then and only then I'll direct you to investigate the ones I find most useful."

Barker next turned a claw-finger to Rufus. "Move your fat ass to the next seat over." A goon face took Rufus's seat. "Better yet just sit over in the corner, so you can't meddle with the downloads."

Rufus conceded his seat, but not his superb hacking skills, which he put to good use after the meeting adjourned. He promised Melanie to bring her something special.

•　　•　　•　　•　　•

That night Rufus visited Melanie, lounging glumly in her living room. He threw open his laptop with the triumphant air of a magician. "Melanie," giggled Rufus. "Cheer up. I hacked into the minister's feed and uncovered scenes from his memories that are in Barker's possession but were not forwarded to our forensic team."

Rufus dialed up the first of two omitted scenes. "Do you want some popcorn, before we begin?" Melanie's lips curled into a wry contortion and stared her answer straight through him.

Rufus conjured up the first scene dating back a week before the terrorist attack. The scene opened with Eric pleading with Barker in his office.

"Listen to me, Barker. I have infiltrated the terrorist group and, by gaining their confidence, learned of their plans to destroy the government nuclear facility." Eric tugged firmly on Barker's shoulder, in order to speak in a low, deliberate voice. "Get this, Barker. The terrorists think I'm a traitor, which works well to my undercover advantage. I've set up a sting operation to bust the terrorists before they attack."

Barker scowled, first in silence. Then he turned abruptly to face Eric. "I can't have you interfere with these attack plans. The terrorists are just hired mercenaries for a plan I orchestrated from the start." Eric's face winced, as Barker threw back his plumage with a wry smile. "You see, Eric, these nuclear facilities counter the Kremlin's strategy to dominate world energy markets, and the Kremlin pays my way. So, I've contracted covertly with a group of Chechen terrorists to cripple US energy output. You are mucking up these plans with your counterintelligence operation." Eric crumpled into his chair, blown away by this revelation, as Barker chided through his pursed beak, "So now you are an unexpected liability." Eric jolted back, stone cold bug-eyed.

"How about this scenario?" mocked Barker. "Eric, the patriot, right? I'll put you smack dab in the middle of this terrorist attack and have you witness the whole thing up close and personal. When the FBI investigates this incident, the government will label you a conspiratorial traitor and allow me to ascend further into the command chain of the American national security apparatus." With that pronouncement a swarm of thugs stormed the room, wrestled Eric to the floor, cuffed him, and whisked him off out of sight.

Blood drained from Melanie's horrified face, but before she spoke, Rufus intruded, "Wait. I have more, and it's eye-popping…excuse the pun." The second scene dates to the day of the attack and looks through Eric's eyes. "See, he is duct taped to a wooden chair, where he is held captive in the apartment overlooking the nuclear facility moments preceding the attack. And look! Before Eric's eyes were gorged out, he shifted his gaze from the window to…guess who? … Barker…. Barker was hovering over him and laughing, as the terrorist burned in the tattoo."

"I can't look at this anymore," decried Melanie, first aghast, then infuriated as the horror unfolded. Melanie and Rufus had succeeded in pealing back the cloak of mystery, but how to notify the team? They agreed. "Let's wait until the next team meeting, to confront Barker."

•　　•　　•　　•　　•

The following morning Melanie and Rufus were ready. Barker had called an impromptu meeting at forensic headquarters to discuss his findings. Quite unceremoniously, he shrugged his vulture shoulders in a quizzical pose, and opened with the following statement, "I have reviewed all the memory downloads from Eric's hybrid avatar, and on the basis of the forensic evidence at hand I have decided to terminate any further investigation into this matter, as none of the downloads contained actionable info."

The forensic team drew a deep sigh of hushed disappointment. Only Melanie broke the group's grieved reverie to address Barker, "We're all so saddened by this unexpected outcome. Moreover, we are all so thankful that you have taken it upon yourself to accept this horrible burden of proof, however repulsive the facts."

Barker cracked a disingenuous smile and let out an all-knowing cackle, "Thank you Melanie. This was a daunting task, and I so appreciate your cooperation." With a dismissive gesture Barker adjourned the meeting with, "Now pardon me. I must tend to urgent matters of national security."

Barker was inching toward the exit, when Melanie popped up and proclaimed with a hint of sarcasm, "Minister Barker, I speak for the team when I said we're so deflated that you could not identify the lead culprit."

Barker feigned resigned relief, saying, "It was probably Stryker… . So disappointing. Like all of us, I cringed at the attack on Eric's eyes, and especially the grisly burning of the terrorist's tattoo into his neck."

Melanie cut off Barker's testimony abruptly and spoke slowly and deliberately, when she said, "Sir, how did you know Eric had his neck tattooed? None of our downloads you gave me showed any tattooing."

Barker stumbled, gazed upon dumbfounded faces, and searched for the exit. Then he turned momentarily to say hesitantly, "Uh…I'm puzzled, Melanie. Why were there no memory feeds to verify something so mentally powerful and memorable?"

"Maybe this will refresh your memory," proclaimed an energized Melanie, as she nodded to Rufus, who unleashed his skittering spider fingers over the computer keys. On cue, a new feed appeared on the wall monitor. Melanie aimed her light pointer at the emerging images and flailed her entire arm to outline the critical elements of the scene.

"This download shows a terrorist tattooing Eric's neck, who is awake and in pain during the procedure." The team gasped in horrified disbelief.

"Barker, my comrade, why was this memory not included in the official records? And how did you know Eric's neck was tattooed, if there were no verification of this in the downloads?" Barker flecked his hawkish eyebrows and accelerated his footsteps to the exit door. Melanie blocked his way, saying with a voice drenched in abject anger, as if she knew Barker could read her mind. "Look, comrade Barker. Is it because this memory feed shows your laughing face staring at the bloody tattoo?" Barker's complexion flushed with this revelation of guilt. He slammed closed his folder and attempted a quickened exit, but he marched into a herd of FBI agents with guns drawn and reciting the standard Miranda rights.

• • • • •

That evening Rufus visited Melanie at her home. With a melancholy glass of wine in her hand, she greeted Rufus gloomily and asked him for anything new. Rufus flipped opened his laptop, while Melanie wandered to the window to gaze out at her pristine garden. "I shared this garden view with Eric on many occasions, but now I know that the last thing he saw was his own death."

"Consider this, Melanie," reassured Rufus. "His own death may not be the last thing Eric sees." Rufus called up the image of the Pacific Island resort on his laptop, where Melanie and Eric hoped to spend private time together.

"If we can mind travel back a week in time before Eric's death, then maybe we could teleport Eric's hybrid avatar forward to a time of your choice." Melanie's countenance brightened, as she nodded consent to Rufus's plan.

"Yes. Let's try it." Rufus hacked into Eric's brain transponder, and tried to redirect it, but, "There's resistance, Melanie." The transponder's bleeping went dead after multiple attempts. Rufus threw up his hands. "I sense some resistance on Eric's part. Maybe he's has had enough…hypnosis?"

"No hypnosis, Rufus," said a dejected Melanie, "but will Eric's hybrid accept this?" Melanie shifted to FaceTime mode, so as to enter Eric's mind with her facial image, and see through his eyes, and he through hers. As if infusing her thoughts into the time transporter, Melanie wished the following, "I love you, Eric. Let me take you to somewhere special." She leaned in with her puckered lips and laid a sticky, ruby red, lipstick kiss stain on the laptop screen. With that, she caressed the keys, and gently touched "Enter."

Soon the fuzzy screen cleared, and images came into sharp focus. Together Melanie and Rufus enjoined Eric's gaze through a window, not of the apartment overseeing the nuclear reactor, but rather that of the Pacific Resort. Through Eric's eyes opened a scene of pristine beauty: balmy breezes combing through swaying palm fronds, layered on the choppy waves of a cobalt blue ocean.

The End

Tail of the Flaming Lion

Campfires are as ancient as the ancient people who built them to welcome the wandering Teller. In those days, as now, when the Teller appeared, even the crickets would hold their chatter. The restless rustle of the darkening forest would hush. The fading sun would bow down, and the star clusters ascending in the dusky African sky would stand in silent testimony. The assembled villagers would whisper in anticipation.

"Lo, the wandering Teller is near!"

Upon his arrival, pungently sweet fragrances would waft from charred cedar embers. Passionate cinder and light beams tinged with burnt ochre rose to bronze the face of the Teller. His bushy, white eyebrows scored his enigmatic, ruddy face, as if seared by an eternal flame. The dancing hands of the Teller, enveloped in the campfire's haze of smoky incense, would stir the primordial soup, spinning off swirling, cosmic clouds of cinder dust. His cloaked presence emerged through the mist at unexpected moments of revelation.

The Teller spoke, "Let there be Light!" We felt his light more than we saw it.

The Teller then threw his hands into the fire, swirling up flame and cinder that burst forth brazenly. Family and friends slumped back with apprehensive trepidation and mesmerized attention to the rocketing display of flame fragments and ash suspended over our heads. In the hands of the Teller, spinning and swirling fragments of congealed ember conjured up the apparition of a flaming lion with its majestic mane, its aggressive claws, its broad, toothy jaw, and its magical tail wavering just beyond our reach. Hovering over the campfire, the lion's glowing body swaggered. Its mane streamed in flickering flames. Its tail curled and waved seductively, as if to tantalize.

"To possess the tail of the Flaming Lion," declared the Teller, "is the sacred prize sought by mortals who dream of eternal life. I knew a man, Matito, who was smitten and consumed by this desire, by the passion to possess the tail of the Flaming Lion." The Teller's hands orchestrated floating fragments of burning cinder so as to recreate before our eyes scenes from the drama of Matito's life. The Teller narrated the story as follows.

"Matito grabbed his spear once more and left his son, Jamburo, and his wife, Kineppi, so that he could wander in the forest and through vast grassy plains for days, weeks, and even months in search of the Flaming Lion. He persevered cold rains and blistering heat. He ignored near starvation.

"Jamburo and Kineppi eked out subsistence from roots and tree gatherings. Jamburo missed his father. He felt forsaken, because he could not share the delights of his growth into manhood in his father's absence. Yet he acquiesced to his father burning desire for immortality. Kineppi soon perished as she succumbed to spiritual starvation for companionship and love.

"Matito had many near encounters with the Flaming Lion over the years. The Lion would creep close to him at night, while Matito was immersed in dreams. The Lion's fiery breath on Matito's body and in his soul only strengthened his conviction to pursue the Lion at all costs. At unexpected moments Matito saw the Lion hiding coyly behind clumps of acacia trees at dawn. The Flaming Lion would tease and flirt with Matito, as if in a private romance, egging him on, which only inflamed his desires.

"Then it happened. One night, under the dim light of the full moon, Matito was crawling on all fours under lush green ferns and fragrant flowers, when the Flaming Lion appeared over his shoulder, puzzled. Seizing his opportunity, Maito grabbed for the elusive tail of the Lion and took possession of it, but the Lion only grinned and salivated. The Flaming Lion sunk his claws deep into Matito's chest and whirled him around playfully. The Lion's fiery jaw then bit down and crushed Matito's head.

"During his remaining moments of life, Matito took no mind of this. He did not think about the crushing of his head. He did not think about his son, who stood till midnight, many nights, hoping that his father would return. He did not think about his wife and her unrewarded devotion. He did not think about his abandoning them to their pitiful, undeserved fates. He did not think about all the years of his lonely isolation.

"Matito thought only of the tail of the Flaming Lion, which he held in his hand at long last. Yet with his last glowing ember of consciousness fading at the precipice of eternity, all Matito saw was his finger poke the eye in the mirror."

The Teller dropped his arms in exhaustion. The magical theatre crumbled and collapsed into the dwindling campfire. Some members of the assembled village had fallen asleep, not fully hearing the story. They would not learn from it.

The Teller clasped his hands and bowed to the few of us still listening. Turning his back on the fading embers, the Teller took his leave back into the lush forest, heading for the next village, carrying in his soul all his sacred tales of mystery and truth.

The End

The Last Portrait of Mighty Mike

Into the musty carpet that covered his bedroom floor Mike's cheek was now buried. The plush pile felt softer than the graveled road upon which Mike crash landed three years ago, after being thrown thirty feet one foggy night by a recklessly speeding car; the night God turned His back on Mike.

He could no better move his feeble arms and legs now than he could when the ambulance arrived. Yet, just moments ago, Mike slouched over the bars of his steely cold wheelchair, straining to reach down and retrieve his younger brother's ID, which lay carelessly under a chair. *That's something my brother might need. I'll get it for him*, thought Mike, animated by his habitually incorrigible impulse to help others. But Mike should have known better than to trust his memory of balance. The Laws of Gravity dragged his indifferent body down harshly onto the floor, like a rumpled sack of fractured dreams, coming to rest in a ludicrously contorted pose, buckled legs splayed and his neck twisted, just as it had been after the accident.

Mike's frantic eyes pulled erratically from side to side before he settled his gaze upon the wall of his bedroom, now awash in the amber tones of the setting sun. He recognized the string of wall-mounted pictures arrayed as portraitures in still life that traced Mike's actual life before the accident.

He imagined himself into the photo with his football buddies. Mike was known as "Mighty Mike," the quarterback who drove his high school team to the championship, and Mike to a full-ride scholarship. He was voted the "Model Student" because he prayed with his team for victory before the game, and prayed for the other team after their defeat.

The crisp, intoxicating aroma of autumnal golden browns infused the wreath, like a crown, that perched on his regal forehead, as he was hoisted aloft on the shoulders of his adoring teammates. In this rarified air of invincibility and grounded in his enduring faith in Providential Goodness and Fairness and Compassion and Charity, he walked blindly, deaf to the screech of impending calamity, as cold as the pavement upon which he had lain.

Evening shadows bled over the family picture of Mike at his graduation with his brother and parents at his side, just hours before Mike pulled over on that drizzly highway, shrouded in murky blackness, to help a stranded traveler.

At office visits, the doctor, I, would press on different spots, and ask, "Does it hurt here, or here, or how 'bout here?"

"Yes," he would say. Then we would schedule future visits to ask the same questions.

With no hope for recovery, Mike became a lonely mind imprisoned in an alien body. His father gave up his job to be his full-time caregiver, because Mike's speech was so unintelligible that only his father could decipher it. His parents divorced, because his mother never forgave his father for allowing Mike to leave home that night. Mike's brother was always angry with Mike, saying, "It's all your fault, you big-hearted clown, for pulling off that desolate highway to help some random stranger. You ruined our family and took my father away from me to be your nursemaid."

Mike's shout to call for his father was muffled by the indifferent carpet. His father did not respond. Mike wondered what his life would become, should his father never return. Mike tried to sleep.

Sleep, Mighty Mike. Sleep and dream about the divine universe, once so grand and glorious.

The End

A Brief History of
Square Pegs in Round Holes

There was a time when peg board games swept the nation. Remember? It's the game whereby the player inserts three-inch-long pegs into holes arrayed on a wooden board. Some of the pegs are long rectangles with square ends, and the others are three-inch-long cylinders with circular ends. The prototypes had all the squares lined up in rows at one end of the board, and the circulars at the other end.

For decades the pegboard game sat idle, collecting dust on distributor's shelves, because the board had a boringly uniform look. Popularity skyrocketed when controversy erupted from toy activists questioning the method of arraying the standard placement restrictions of pegs on the board, claiming it was too polarizing for children. Others claimed passionately that certain of the square pegs might self-identify as circular pegs, and wanted them to be placed in the rows along with square pegs. Others wanted square and circular pegs to be distributed in a more socially equitable pattern over the board, preferably six inches apart, and that areas within the board should be proportional with a more equal mix of circular and square pegs.

The debate over the appropriate method of integrating the pegs became heated with opposing voices becoming increasingly aggressive. Police were called urgently to mediate disputes, when, for example, neighbors would mount flags featuring square pegs over their driveways in neighborhoods favoring round pegs. Peg riots broke out in many cities across America, so politicians redlined new peg-friendly districts.

When the manufacturers recommended using a heavy hammer to violently force square pegs into round holes, rights activists at the ACLU took the manufacturers to court. Finally, the issue was decided by the Supreme Court in a close 5/4 decision, favoring the consumers. Representing the majority position the Chief Justice held the manufacturers in contempt of Diversity, Inclusion, and Equity, and ordered the manufacturers to make the appropriate accommodations to integrate the pieces. Reparations were awarded to the plaintiffs in the form of refunds plus pain and suffering.

The manufacturers tried to accommodate varied consumers demands by designing pegs square on one side and round on the other. Yet some countered that this resulted in too many of one peg type, but not enough of the other hole type. Manufacturers then mixed square and circular features at branch points along the peg, so that each peg could insert into more than one type of adjacent hole. Unfortunately, consumers found the game had become too complex and confusing. Further, the assimilation attempt caused pieces to lose their original identities. The game dropped in popularity, and eventually most of the pegboards were burned in public bonfires across the nation.

Years later, nostalgic collectors across the nation would take their pegboard games out of storage for a yearly pegboard parade to commemorate the history of attempted pegboard integration. Many wore T-shirts showing square pegs or round pegs, but none with both, embarrassing the parade organizers. Gargantuan pegboards, the size of a football field, were constructed by the government for pegs of all types in public parks, at taxpayer expense. Coming full circle, man-ufacturers reaped huge profits from these ostentatious public displays. Sated activists moved onto cancel other pressing issues on social media.

83

The End

Security Question # 5

"Just tell my attorney that I got my Username and Password correct, but I screwed up on security question number five, you know, the one that asks you about your most embarrassing moment ever."

He scratched his balding scalp, rolled his shifty eyes, and explained, "Okay, I nailed the first four security questions, no sweat." He held up fingers to list them one by one.

#1. Which of your toes is the longer? The first or second? Check, correct.

#2. What's your favorite place to expose yourself in public? Check, correct.

#3. Where did you hide your whiskey bottles from your ex-wife? Check, correct.

#4. How many times did you lie on your tax statements to cover a gambling debt? Check, correct.

Check, check, check, and check. BUT, when I fumbled over security question number five—the most embarrassing question of all—I flunked. Why? It's complicated, so I need to explain.

I started out by recalling the time I nearly missed my connecting flight at Heathrow. Bolting down the gangway, I saw the plane inching away from the dock with the cabin door still open. So, I leapt, miss the landing, but managed to cling to the cabin doorframe by my fingertips, my body and legs dangling over the tarmac.

The flight attendant insisted on boarding verification, so, freeing up a hand, I pulled out my cell phone to show them the flight bar code. They rejected it, because the bar code was for a previous junket to Las Vegas (that my ex-wife didn't know about). So, I flipped the screen to another bar code, but that only certified my purchase of some marijuana gummies.

Meanwhile, the airplane was taxiing faster and faster. There was jet fuel in my face, and I couldn't see, because this long, thin paper in my breast pocket was flapping against my face. I yanked it out, and, lo and behold, it's my boarding pass waving in the breeze. The flight attendants took their sweet time to clear me, after some extended discussion with air traffic control, and then dragged my sorry ass through the narrow cabin door, just as the plane was about to lift off.

That's when I lost my right shoe. So, here's where it gets weird.

When I got to LAX, I was so mortified walking about the terminal with one bare foot that I pulled the Dodger cap down over my eyes, but then I hit my head hard on the doorframe of the public toilet. I staggered all around, just as a gaggle of angry ladies were leaving the bathroom in a huff. I swore that one of the security guards jumped me, but when I swung back, I smashed in the nose of this big dude with a weird gang tattoo on his neck. Embarrassing, right?

So, I entered this story into the security computer program for question number five, but the computer rejected it, as if I were withholding some other embarrassing moment that I didn't fess up to. I wracked my brain. Was it the time that I dressed up in my wife's lingerie at the very moment my kids came home? Or was it the time I texted my girlfriend with lewd comments after midnight but dialed my wife's cell number by accident?

The prison guard nudged my shoulder to put down the microphone and step away from the cubicle. Marching back to my jail cell, I momentarily turned to shout to my attorney, "Just tell my ex-wife everything I said, except about the gummies!"

So, wouldn't you know it, when I swung back around, I slammed into this big angry dude with a weird gang tattoo on his neck.

The End

Waves of Snowdrifts

Michael and Jimmy were inseparable. As brothers, their love for each other was "as deep as the ocean," jested Jimmy, as he and Michael cruised jovially that night, floating on smooth and placid seas.

As cruel fate would have it, no sooner had they toasted with the clink of after-dinner Cognac glasses, and without forewarning, both were swept off the deck of the cruise liner and swallowed up by the unexpected intrusion of a ravenous, murky, and petulant sea.

Searchlights, beaming from rescue boats, crisscrossed to scour for survivors. Flashes of lights, illuminating the human carnage, skipping from dismembered guests to old men guzzling down their last gulp of salty brine, to mothers, frantically scooping with arms immersed in oily slick to reach their wailing children.

The massive propeller blade at the rear of the sinking cruise liner ascended and whirled, driving down mightily the fractured hulk into the turbulent waters. Dismayed passengers were propelled in their cabins upward into the godless sky. At sea level the captain commanded the rescue boat, yelling, "Row, row, row. The engine's gonna blow!"

Michael extended a hand to grasp the edge of the rescue boat and then a lifeline hand to Jimmy bobbing just out of reach. "Now roooooooow!" urged the captain. As the rescue boat surged forward, Micheal's and Jimmy's hands came undone. Jimmy bobbed like a helpless, unmoored buoy and sank beneath white-capped waves. A flash of lightning illuminated Jimmy's anguished face, just moments before he vanished into the recesses of memory.

• • • • •

Michael's sympathetic wife, Chelsea, understood and soothed Michael's grief, but Chelsea had always been a restless sleeper, who often tossed and turned unexpectedly.

One night, months after Jimmy's passing, her flailing arm jolted Michael right out of his nightmarish sleep. He was immersed in salty sweat and gasped for air in the drafty darkness of his bedroom, in the pitch darkness of a snow-stormy night.

He staggered down darkened hallways, bumbling awkwardly, dizzy and queasy. He passed the bedroom, where Jimmy's children now slept in peaceful silence. He relived the pounding thrust of imaginary waves, which stoked his urge to rescue them once again.

The flash of a lightbulb cut through the shadows and drew Michael's focus to an illusory specter of Jimmy's frantic body. Michael followed the apparition, as it slid passed him and down the hallway, seemingly on the crest of an invading sea swell. Michael turned from this horrific vision, and, as before, shut an imaginary cabin door.

"I had to save the children and myself," Michael repeated to himself again and again.

Michael leaned forward and pressed his palms and forehead against the cold windowpane that overlooked his wintry backyard. Swells of tall, arching snowdrifts posed like grasping ghostly fingers. The pinwheel atop the children's monkey bars spun mindlessly.

Michael unlocked the deadbolt of the door to his backyard. He braced himself against the frigid gusts of snow that splashed and lashed mercilessly against his cheeks, already moistened with tears.

An eerier, ghostly visage of Jimmy's wistful spirit bobbed and heaved on a sea of slush, only to vanish again into the white-capped waves of snowdrifts.

Michael lowered his head, and, seeking atonement, he whispered, "It should have been me. It should have been me."

The End

Most Precious Possession

Chelsea inhaled the warm, doughy fragrance of freshly salted pretzels pleated into the pungent plumes of exhaust fumes that permeated the Greyhound bus terminal. With valise in tow, she shoved through a jumble of cantankerous strangers, jostling raucously across the station platform.

In a flash Chelsea caught an instantaneous image of her girlish self in the windowpane of the bus: she, with her hasty scarf, a shabby pullover yanked defiantly from the hall closet, and a sticky dew drop clinging stubbornly to the corner of her eye.

Turning abruptly to catch the 7:15 in Bay 16, she inadvertently swung her valise directly into the oncoming valise of a careless stranger. Her contents spewed far and wide. Within a moment, the indifferent, glossy black of the platform floor became a cacophonous pageant of Chelsea's life: pressed flowers skittering out of her wedding album; a necklace gifted her by her adulteress husband; the memorial speech at her father's graveside; an apology note she never mailed to her estranged mother.

"Is this some sort of prank?" barked Chelsea, avoiding eye contact with the *idiot stranger*. She dropped to her knees and scurried about to recapture the tokens of her former life. To her horror, all her sentimentalities had been kicked away by the stampede of callous strangers trampling over remnants of her life's path.

In the commotion of the moment, she casually gazed upward to study the face of the reprehensible trickster. To her amazement, the face of the stranger looked eerily familiar. Standing up, Chelsea studied the face of the stranger up close. His smile and knowing wink opened Chelsea's eyes widely, for she was staring into the face of her cousin, Michael. Chelsea's cheeks fever flushed with a deeper hue of crimson than any envious rouge could ever hope to surpass.

"Oh my God, Michael," exclaimed Chelsea with a quivering, giddy voice. "I can't believe it's you, after all these years. You left me no clue."

Chelsea returned to her panicked retrieval efforts, pleading, "I must find it, Michael. You know, the photo portraits of us as children at summer camp, so many years ago. We were so close then, when we unburdened our young hearts. Please help me find my copy."

Michael reached into his breast pocket. With the finesse of the whimsical magician who guards all unexpected surprises, he pulled out an old, faded Polaroid, and asked, "Do you mean this?"

The End

Before We Say Goodnight

Norma rejoiced at the opportunity to set the dinner table, because her daughter requested she do so. Her fingers, aged, veiny, crooked, and liver-spotted, grasped the flatware as tenaciously as she had held onto her children for as long as she could.

The dinner table was populated with Santa Claus figurines and mangers, a display as bright and cheery as any Christmas before. She set to work: all the forks, tines up to the left; all the spoons and all the knives, like parent/child pairings, were assigned to the right. Then, all the bread plates to the left corner and all the teacups, face down to the right corner. *There, there, and there.* Each plate was centered and framed like a family portrait in balanced togetherness.

Norma nodded inwardly. *No one wants to endure the loneliness of something out of place or forgotten.* A silver-grey filigree of curls caressed her furrowed forehead over watchful eyes that gazed beyond the dinner table into the distant past. In that suspended state of inner vision, she felt hollowed out, despite her joyous stride to place the blueberry pie among the table's festive display.

Then up sprung good old George, chuckling as he spied Norma's rituals. He reached toward the table settings, extending stubby, obstinate fingers from hands accustomed to grasping decisively. He scooped up capriciously a family of flatware from their designated positions and clumped them whimsically in a pile at the center of the holiday display.

"No need to fret over things that don't matter, I always say," proclaimed George with his trademark mocking smirk, once employed effectively in business but, since retirement, was repurposed for jovial conviviality.

Norma pivoted to George. Her silent glare, more of a scowl, seared into George's impudent eyes like laser beams, one for each candle on his birthday cake. She reset the violated flatware.

"Oh, Momma. I see you've already met George, even before I made the proper introductions," said Norma's daughter with the beaming face of a child showing off her first finger painting. "George retired from a lucrative business that he commanded for forty years. He's quite accomplished." Then she bent furtively toward Norma's ear, whispering under her breath discretely by barely moving her lips. "He's available and a real 'lady's man,' Momma."

George intruded clumsily. "I was named Businessman of the Year in 1984," he touted, "and finished third in five Ironman contests in the 1970 Olympic trials." He concluded his peroration with a stylized knightly bow that either naively miscalculated or more likely stupidly parodied a theatrical depiction of humility, in Norma's opinion. George then tucked his shirttails over his bulging belly and gimped on a bad knee to collapse into an easy chair.

Like rings of an old, gnarly tree trunk, thought Norma, observing the deep crevices that scored George's weathered face. She might tolerate his fictions, however real and glorious they appeared to him, but *there was no athlete left in him. And he was no all- star at love, either.* She knew that, too.

"So, how do you like retiring from your former self?" chided Norma, lying down a trap pregnant with ironic sarcasm. "Still full steam ahead?"

"That's funny you say it in that way," confessed George with a wilting smile. An edgy silence grew between them, until George came forth and spoke with wistful inflection, seeming no longer addressing Norma's ears alone.

"I have a dream every night," he confessed. "I see myself on a locomotive barreling down the tracks, speeding through fields of color, just a blur." George used his hands to create the scene. "Now, I'm going and going, and the colorful blur just whizzes by, but the tracks never end." George reached out to grip the air. "See, I'm reaching for it, but it's always beyond my grasp." George squeezed Norma's shoulders, while his lips quivered. "Then, there's another dream. I'm staring out the window to view the colorful fields, while seated in a plush leather couch of the lounge coach, where my partners and I chat and play Blackjack over cigars and Cognac on the day when the senior partner up and threw his cards in my face, and swore he would avenge all that he perceived as cunning!"

Norma turned her face away from George, so as to not see further into his troubled soul. She put aside her feud for a moment. At a loss for words, she fiddled with the upper edge of her blouse, bunching it around her neckline. This drew George's attention to the layers of sagging flesh suspended from her wrinkled and painted face.

Youth and Beauty had gone and was not coming back, thought George. *She fooled no one. The vitality of motherhood had run its course, too. Her children had likely established lives of their own. She probably saved the toys and books she used to read to them in bed, until she felt embarrassed one day when she found herself unwelcome as an intimate in their youthful circles. She probably cried like an abandoned child when her last drove off. They no longer needed her to wipe their runny noses or hug them to sleep. She's a lonely, hollowed out visitor in their homes, where she smiles through her tears.* George could see that, too.

Hoping to resuscitate George from his distractions, Norma inserted herself. "Maybe the fields of color in your dreams are fields of flowers. I love flowers in bloom." Norma made eye contact, saying, "I have dreams like you, George, of colorful fields, where I gather luscious flowers into lovely bouquets. Each flower has a name…and a voice…. and a joyous squeal of astonished laughter, like when a Christmas gift appears miraculously from the spirit of love that permeated our home. Like the sweet fragrance of flowers in bloom." Norma gazed to her aging hands and continued hesitantly. "Yet, in my dreams, the luscious flowers, when held in my embrace, wilt and wither away. My arms are empty again."

George's austere countenance softened and his shoulders rounded. He sensed her sadness and longing as he had never before sensed in another. He knew he was longing, too, but he just stood there immobilized, silently staring at the edge of the table, as if still peering out of the coach lounge window, abandoned by partners, who left without looking through the window at the blur of colors, that now came into focus on the floral centerpiece of the table at which Norma was standing. He picked up a rose from the bouquet, delicately, presenting it to Norma, his other hand caressing her shoulder.

"Why, thank you, sir. Thank you," said Norma, whose expression bloomed, her cheeks blushing crimson. Norma made a proposal. "We should visit together the fields of color in our dreams. Maybe that's where the train tracks end."

"And maybe we will find some fine flowers there that bloom just for you," intoned George.

The diner party was just getting into full swing, when Norma and George left early and together.

The End

ONE LAST REQUEST, PLEASE

We pulled over to the side of the road, when something went thump, thump under the wheels of our car. My father was the first out, but all of us kids spilled into the street to join the investigation. There was nothing there except for some roadkill at a distance back. We sallied up to the dead bird to take a closer look.

The roadkill splayed out like an untamed still life, frozen in time; talons curled in secret preparedness; wings unfurled, as if still free in flight; a worm hung from its beak, as if celebrating a meal, perhaps even a catch to feed its young. Its eviscerated guts lay fully exposed, no longer concealing its private soul. Its eyes, now darkened, sunk deep, and seemed to look inward, transfixed, and inaccessible. Decay had begun. Who could know how long before the story of this roadkill becomes indecipherable?

We entered the funeral parlor. Redolent whiffs of sanctimonious incense, mingling with cleansing disinfectant and fumes of spilled embalming fluid, wafted like ethereal spirits throughout the chapel. At the center of it all was Grandpa, eased in final repose from an sudden death; sunken eyes and hollowed cheeks. He even looked smaller, as if he were already sinking into oblivion; his once pounding life force crashing through a wave, now drained away like the tide's edge receding over dry sand on a desolate beachhead.

Yet for all who had the misfortune of knowing him, Grandpa was a flagrantly unrepentant misanthrope and irascible curmudgeon. Famously, when asked what he wanted on his tombstone, he ranted with his trademark pugnacious temerity, "Humanity is just a festering carbuncle of cantankerous pus, clinging to a crusty speck of galactic debris, that floats aimlessly through the cold, dark void of the incorrigibly indifferent universe." During the Christmas party, he'd be holed up alone in his room. All felt relieved with his passing.

The priest, cloaked in a flowing black robe, which covered his head in a drooping hoody, presided over the testimonials. He brought the gathering to order by striking rhythmically, hypnotically, a bong and chimes, which entraining our eyes into a trance of smoky incense frothing from a swinging challis.

"If no one wants to speak on Grandpa's behalf, then let Grandpa emerge from death and into this room to testify in his own behalf. Shall we?" The priest rolled his eyes skyward, so that only the whites of his eyes could be seen. He raised the forefinger and pinky of each hand to form the image of two divining rods. "Come out, Grandpa, come out of you seclusion one more time and speak your peace."

With that pronouncement, the priest distributed Oculus headsets as Grandpa's advanced directive required, surprising us with this odd one last request. Each headset was equipped for virtual reality viewing, complete with olfactory air compressors and sensory gloves. We strapped them on, and, to our amazement, as if in a trance, a strange scene in Metaverse magically unfolded.

Immersed in a vast expanse of serene misty blueness, undulating and shimmering along the edges, ghostly shadows floated upward. We shaded our burning eyes from staring into the blindingly brilliant celestial firmament.

In the distance, an approaching object floated into view. To our utter amazement it was Grandpa reclining on a gilded couch, inlaid with diamonds and other precious stones. Before him was a banquet of milk and honey, and cradling him was a lush garden of richly deep greens and exquisitely fragrant flowers. The fine texture of his ruddy face was radiant and his eyes blazed. His iridescent cotton-puff of white hair and luminous gown ebbed and flowed with gentle gusts of balmy breezes. Grandpa reached out to us graciously with choreographed gestures that seemed natural and effortless. We could feel the press of his flesh against the gloves of our hands.

"Grandpa," I blurted out innocently. "Where are you?"

"I am in Heaven," Grandpa replied with a gracious smile that we had not seen for years. His facial features and idiosyncratic physical gestures were so real, so fresh and spontaneous that, to our perception, IT WAS GRANDPA, himself, right in front of us, as real as real can be, reaching out to us from the Great Beyond.

"Dear children, I rejoice to be with you once more," said Grandpa whose smile momentarily radiated sincere jubilation until his expression abruptly transfigured. He averted his gaze into empty space and hung his head.

"Please listen to my confession," pleaded Grandpa. "Shortly before my passing I awoke one night with my heart thumping from a horrible realization." A desperate and grim shadow washed over Grandpa's now ashen countenance.

"All my life I was devoted to you, my children. Every conscious moment I was in perpetual flight from one obligation to another, so as to provide for you, my family. Caught up in the pressures of the day, I failed to be present in the precious moments with you and express my deepest feelings. I had so much to tell you that I could not say. Anger and regret were my daily companions. My gaze turned inward to self-loathing and disappointment, which only intensified my isolation. I bare my soul to you now, poised, as I am, at the precipice of eternal banishment, to plead with you for forgiveness." Aghast, we all offered Grandpa a moment of silence. His eyes delved inaccessibly inward, as he fell to the ground and knelt at our feet, sobbing bitterly.

Then, in a flash, his solemn revelation unraveled, as he spoke anew in harsher, savage tones through gnashed teeth that belied his hellishly tortured soul.

"Tell me you will forgive my indifference," he implored. "I must have your forgiveness!" Grandpa clawed at us, as if possessed with the twitchy talons of a bird unjustly fallen from the sky. The priest clicked his fingers three times, and the trance abruptly vanished. We ripped off our headsets, as the celestial Metaverse evaporated.

Our family of pallbearers gathered somberly in silence to lay Grandpa's coffin to rest. All was forgiven. The sun shone brightly on the metallic shovel with which each of us sprinkled with care and respect a soothing blanket of soil onto Grandpa's bedded coffin. Clambering back to the car and speeding away, we felt no thump, thump. The roadkill had vanished.

The End

The Testaments of Dinah and Tamar

1. Dinah

"Did you see the look of shock on Shechem's face, when my sword came in unto him?" Levi aped with ribald arabesque the artful lunging of his saber. The assembly of members roared raucously in response. As if glowing with divine approval, radiant shafts of ethereal light illuminated the stately arches, billowing flags and streamers in the tabernacle of the Brotherhood. "And, Lo, there was Hamor, witnessing his son croak right in front of him, all the while hopping about and holding his own bloody dick in his hands." Another roar bellowed from the rowdy congregation.

"Simeon, get up herein and tell the brothers about how you broughteth woe to the Hivites who defiled our sister, Dinah, therein." Simeon took center stage, bringing the brothers in close for the story.

"All right, guys. Remember how Shechem defileth our sister, Dinah, right? Thinking he could capture her in a fake marriage bondage, so as to defile her again and again, expecting we would all just ignore it and make nice together, our two peoples, peaceable and all, forfeiting our prized women to that heathen abomination?"

Simeon whispered to draw them in closer. "Behold, I got this brainstorm. A little trick I concocted to humbleth their hubris. I spake unto Shechem to make a deal: have all the men of his tribe geteth circumcised first, you know, to appear God fearing, ostensibly as a prerequisite before our pledge to mingle with these degenerates afterwards. So, he actually bought into it and gathered all the men in their tribe to convince them to cut off the foreskin of their dicks." A huge roar of laughter belched forthwith.

Simeon wagged a gnarly finger and pronounced, "But goeth unhappy is the man who curseth our Lord and for whom the Lord spoils and correcteth."

"Now, here's where it gets interesting. On the third day," Simeon stuttered as he caught himself giggling. " Picture this. These guys were busy holding their dicks in pain, right? So, Levi and I, along with a few brothers, sneaked uponeth them, and *surprise*! We stabbed to death all the Hivite men on the spot and took captive of their women and cattle. Why? Because they were an abomination in the eyes of the Lord! Oh, man, what easy spoils." The brothers doubled over in tearful laughter over Simeon's reveling LOL moment, and Simeon savored it all.

The roar yielded to respectful silence, as all eyes were then riveted on Jacob, who emerged into the tabernacle and wendeth a path through the congregation and up to the bimma. Jacob surveyed the gathered brethren, as did Abraham the Promised Land, his eyes touching each man approvingly; each man anointed, each man an heir to the sacred privileges as the Brotherhood of the Chosen. The refined texture of his face and sparkling eyes were matched only by the glitter of bracelets of diamonds and precious stones, the talismanic signet ring, and the singular Staff, all symbols of his divine authority and moral compass. The celestial light that Jacob stepped into ignited the radiance of his cottony white hair and golden robe that ebbed and flowed, as if caressed by gentle gusts of balmy breezes that descended from the Eternal.

Jacob set himself to speaketh with supreme authority, "God hath given us dominion therein over all creation. Rightly so. As Simeon and Levi have pointed out, our dominion would include our women, of course, whom God derived from us, our rib, and had given us as our gift to be bartered with therein. Rightly so. The female offspring extend us into the divine future with an eternal lineage, which is our sacred duty and privilege, as promised by Abraham. So, it *WAS* an affront to our brotherhood, all of our righteous women, and as a curse to the Almighty, when Dinah ran from her divine duties and defiled herself and our entire community. Dishonor demands retribution, agreed. There is no place in the land of Abraham for defilers." Whooping and cheers exploded from the congregation.

Jacob grasped his staff with whitened knuckles and thrust it upward, proclaiming with a mighty voice, "As leader of our sacred tribe and guardian of our Lord's Will, my divine responsibility is to preserve God's order and our lineage."

"But what about the whore, Dinah, the harlot?" demurred the many voices in the throng.

"The problem of the harlot is a perplexing issue," bemoaned Jacob, as his dubiety drifted into introspection. "I will need to know the ways of the Divine in this manner of sacrilege, and to prepare for, and, nay, punish harlots who defile us."

2. Tamar

It wasn't often that one of the women of the tribe was summoned to the tent of Judah after dark. Rumors murmuring about Tamar were unconfirmed. Prudently, Tamar, widow of Judah's son, the deceased Er, and then his brother, the deceased Onan, approached the tent of Judah with trepidation. Alone, but not intimidated, Tamar hid her joyless face behind one of her many mundane scarves designed to mask her identity, as was the tradition of invisible women.

A mischievous, ghostly gale of desert wind rent open a flap in the sacred tent. Tamar gazed toward the tall shadows of the tabernacle dedicated to the Brotherhood. A belch of suffocatingly stale air forced upon her a repulsive stench of pungent male body sweat and frankincense.

The veil of secrecy now lifted, the inner sanctum of Judah's tabernacle was revealed. Upwards was a flourish of unsheathed swords that projected downward menacingly from the rafters, like the teeth of a wolf. Tamar spied Judah, sulking on his royal throne with Simeon commiserating at his side. The searing torches positioned behind his throne eclipsed Judah in silhouetted darkness. The same illumination ironically cast a flickering, orange patina over Tamar's statuesque pose, like an apparition, an augury, about which Tamar was not yet prescient.

"Did you call for me, my lord?" asked Tamar with measured speech, but without a flinch of subordination. Judah gazed sharply at Tamar. His countenance morphed into a sneer of disgust. He propped himself up aggressively, pointing a gnarly finger at Tamar, and began unceremoniously, "Hast thou with child?"

"Not as we speak, my lord."

Simeon catapulted to his feet and paced the floor heatedly. "I had heard that thou hast forbidden Onan from placing his seed within you."

"Nay, my lord," asserted Tamar, whose wry lips curled without even a hint of atonement. "Onan had cometh into me many times, my Lord, but he preferred to leaveth his seed upon the dirt therein," stated Tamar quite casually.

Simeon's pacing accelerated, as he snarled, "I have heard from some of the women that you squirmeth and howl with wild, malefic incantations, so as to wrencheth thyself away from Onan and Er to avoid their seed, to killeth his God-given lineage."

Judah interceded, "God's Will is crystal clear, Tamar. When there is a death of a husband, the lineage of the family, nay, the tribe is propagated through the seed of his brother, so that our women's lives, loyalty, and commitments are tied forever to their husband's families through their husband's offspring, through Onan's, Er's brother, in your case. Onan was instructed by the Almighty to raiseth up seed in place of his brother. Onan was aware of the threat of God's wrath, because the voluntary spilling of his seed was wicked in the eyes of the Lord consequent to defiance of God's Will. God sleweth my sons in His displeasure, first Er and then Onan, as punishment, when in actuality God should have taken you, Tamar, to punisheth your trickery and evil ways! You had been commanded to be a receptacle to spawn our family's lineage, but instead your sin puteth my sons' lives at risk."

"My lords, pardon my boldness," asserted Tamar firmly, tight-lipped and wide-eyed. "My receptacle is more than a repository for lease. It is the floret of my flower."

Judah and Simeon were baffled by her defense, but undeterred in their aggressive response, Simeon shouted, "Put her to the sword! She is the devil, who bringeth evil into our midst, and who knows who will be her next victim."

"Our lineage taketh precedence," proclaimed Judah. "I have no choice other than to holdeth you in our house, in shameful mourning, for your deceased husbands, until the day comes, when my youngest son, Sheleah, is of sufficient age to enter you, therein impregnating you with the seeds of his brothers and continue our lineage. You will taketh on the blackened garb of the widow, and remaineth in my house, until Sheleah comes of age. So be it."

3. Cave of the Adullamite

It came to pass that Judah's wife passed to Sheol, and Judah was lonely. To raiseth his spirits he wenteth up to Timnath for the sheep-shearing holiday. Concordantly, Tamar grasped her opportunity to escape, and she slipped out of the house of Judah as a penurious waif, still wearing the blackened garb of the widow. She fledeth forthwith to the cave of the Adullamite.

Tamar was an indigent in the land of Abraham, where the sun rejoiceth in the word of God, but for Tamar the sun created for her barely a shadow. The formidable, ancient mountains guarding the distant horizon stood firm and unmovable beyond which the edge of the known world met eternity.

Carrying the heavy burden of the widow's garb through the barren desert, Tamar persevered the laborious journey to the Adullamite cave. Once she arrived, relief from the searing heat of oppression was assuaged by the cool and inviting darkness in the womb of the cave, a cave too dark even for the eyes of God.

With buoyant steps she penetrated the sanctuary, awe inspired and enchanted by the ancient stalactites suspended from the roof of the cave. The holy sanctuary was pregnant with fragrant alcoves, mysterious and fallopian with promise, and studded with diamonds, rubies, and sapphires. A singular shaft of light pierced the celling of the tabernacle and illuminated a pool of deep blue water at her feet. Tamar bent her knees to refresh herself.

Playfully she swished the water freely with her hands, creating a kaleidoscopic display of colorful ripples. As the turbulence settled, she gazed into the still water's depths, where the image of another woman's face reflected back at her. Tamar recognized the image of Dinah, who, Tamar had heard, had been the renegade who defiled the tribe years ago.

"Tamar," spoke Dinah, "I have a story to tell you about a woman, Miriam, who lived long ago into the future." Tamar smiled broadly to rejoice in the voice of another lonely and isolated sister with whom she could commune. Dinah began her narration, while the images in the frothy pool again rippled and transfigured.

"At the moment of creation, the Old Man, God eternal, emerged from the darkness, and set to work on Creation. For his crowning achievement he fashioned hands and feet, and to the head he affixed a yarmulke, a scraggly beard and long hair extensions, that muffled their ears. He made man in His own image, His own likeness, His own attitude. He called these humans, Hamans, because they were the privileged sons of God.

"As a final step He swirled His sacred gragger, from which poured a heavenly shower of poppy seeds that breathed life into the Hamans. The Hamans were very appreciative. So, to remain in good standing, they prayed to Him all day with exuberant praise, genuflection and sacred vocalizations.

"Soon, the Hamans became bored and needy, and they complained to the Old Man, He. Having heard their kvetching, He conjured up another creation. Derived from a discarded, purposeless rib, new bodies were fashioned, female in shape and countenance, weak and submissive constitutions, but shrouded in greyness and mystery. They became the Others. They were created to fulfill the imagination of men.

"The Others were put to work to serve the Hamans, caring for their every need. For while the Hamans were busy praying, the Others had to cook, clean, prepare the home, bear the children, rear them alone, sit alone in Schul, be silent, and obey compliantly. If these eight plagues were not enough, worst of all, the Hamans made them do unspeakable acts at night in private. The Hamans had uncontestable dominion over the Others.

"The chief Haman was the neediest and most arrogant of them all, because he was so blindly self-absorbed. He alone among the Hamans possessed the greatest power over the Others, who were resigned to their lowly position, except Miriam. She objected to the enslavement of her fellow Others. The Hamans ridiculed her and resisted with threats.

"Then, as if by a miracle, while singing to rally her sisters, from Miriam's mouth issued forth a fountain of sacred water that showered and refreshed all of her sister slaves. Their life colors grew bright and their minds animated. The flood of water also washed over poppy seeds, that transformed into small oranges, that grew bigger and bigger by the moment, as they floated into the sky.

"Fearful about something out of their control, the Hamans cried out for help. So, the Old Man, He, emerged from the darkness again, and said, 'It was not good.' Yet, Miriam tricked him. She floated up a huge orange over Him, and squashed it down from the crown of His head to the nap of His neck. He struggled to remove it but could not wrench the orange off His head. Then the orange split miraculously and pealed back, revealing the face of a Goddess with benevolent eyes and an indomitable passion for Justice.

"One huge orange peel then fell from Her head and crushed the chief Haman below. The other Hamans could not hide from the oranges, so they became domesticated and learned to behaveth themselves. All the Others became sisters, who did not need Hamans to live a good life."

As the kaleidoscopic images in the turbulent pool dissipated, the wings of doves washed through the cave on balmy breezes and swirled lovingly about Tamar.

"I have a lofty vision for you, Tamar," extolled Dinah. "A grand scheme for your eyes only. You must know by now that Judah's promise to you, to tie you to the will of his son, Shelah, was a lie. If you return, you will be fated to the invisible life of women as captive and prisoner. You must now assert your freedom by breaking with the rules of Judah."

Tamar's consciousness dove deep, and from the recesses of her creative mind she conjured up a wild and brilliant machination. "To set myself free I must take from Judah his symbols of power, authority, self-righteousness, and privilege. But all with which I have to gamble is that which make me valuable as a woman in his eyes."

Dinah agreed. "But for every harlot there is a willing collaborator, who hides in the darkness, shrouded in the secret company of ignominy. Harlotry may be the only path to reveal the Truth, Tamar. Trap him in his own hypocrisy."

Tamar pulled off her widow's garments. She wrapped herself in a sensuous gown of orange hue to attract Judah's attention. A facial veil of anonymity completed the outfit and set the trap.

4. ROAD TO TIMNATH

Tamar was drawneth to the bustling marketplace situated on the dusty road to Timnath, where businessmen and entrepreneurs hustled their overpriced goods and services. Tamar situated herself in plain view along the roadside. Her bright orange gown sparkled like a golden calf, advertising her preparedness to deal.

As Judah approached Tamar's location on the destitute side of the road, his vision fixated on what seemed to him to be a needy waif in orange cloak. He smiled with the thought that the waif could be a divine gift for a lonely old man. Judah sat down beside Tamar, who seemed not to notice him. She turned her face away from his enamored gaze to fully mask her true identity.

Tamar did not want Judah to know just then about her private anger, her secret enmity, and her anguished travail. She was hoping to play Judah's overtures as a prelude to combat in this man's game of power and dominance. Tamar breathed the air of a free woman in the marketplace, where cunning, deception, and conquest were the ways of men.

Judah, smitten by her allure, spoke sweetly, professing his overwhelming attraction to her. "My dear Judah," cooed Tamar in response. "It's, ah…Judah, is it?" Tamar twirled Judah's long hair extensions, as Judah nodded sheepishly. Tamar opened, "I'm sure we can find an accommodation and strike a deal to helpeth little old me with my unfortunate situation here on the destitute side of the road." Tamar doubled down on her sultry voice, saying, "I am so attracted to your virility, Judah, that I feel overwhelmed by your mere presence." At this point Tamar separated her knees ever so slightly, pretending that Judah was not looking. "Perhaps we could strike a deal to assure our future engagements." Judah was already breathless.

"I will need collateral to seal our collaboration," cautioned Tamar, as she turned closely to Judah's quivering lips. "If you are not able to pay now for my excellent services, then perhaps you could give me a pledge, a token, of your commitment to my welfare, and who knows where this will lead." Tamar clasped Judah's cheeks in the palms of her hands and asked, "What wilt thou giveth me that thou wilt seal thine pledge?"

Judah eyed Tamar with his chin up, gaze downward, and professed condescendingly, "I am a wealthy and powerful but cautious man. For now, I am prepared to offer you a goat, which will sustain you until our next affaire de coeur. At this moment I do not have the goat, but my pledge and good name are pristine."

As if just now thinking of it, and pretending it to be an afterthought, Tamar brightened up, saying, "Perhaps, Judah, you could leave your staff and signet ring with me. I will be a good custodian of them in your absence, for they have no value to me." Judah dropped his staff, bracelets, and signet rings, and then revealed his circumcision.

•　　•　　•　　•　　•

Several days later, Judah's friend, the Adullamite, was concerned about Judah's unusual self-absorption and preoccupation, saying, "Judah, why so glumeth?" Truth be told, Judah had retreated to ponder his circumstances, reflecting on his shameful escapade with the Harlot in Timnath. He was fearful of a scandal, should the harlot not be paideth off.

"Here," said Judah, pointing to a scrawny goat. "Of the pair take this second goat, the Azazel she-goat, and deliver it to the harlot at the side of the road in Timnath. Don't forget to collect all that she owes me. Then send her on her way."

Several days later the Adullamite returned to Judah the she-goat, and with puzzled and incredulous intonation confessed, "No harlot was found in Timnath,, and none seems to have existed, according to locals."

Subsequently, Judah was plagued by anxious ruminations whenever mixing amongst the tribe. To raise himself above suspicion, Judah avoided questions about the whereabouts of his signet ring and staff. To deflect scandal, he wove stories ranging from mundane excuses to complex extenuating circumstances, all the while furtively anxious that others might catch on to the inventive flavor infusing his narratives. In the darkness of his tent Judah prayed through the night. He knelt to stroke the she-goat, the Azazel, to absolve his sins, and then sent the goat into the wilderness to seek purgation. The Adulla-mite said, "Woe becometh the man who does not owneth his sins but purges them in the scapegoat therein."

5. Trial of the Whore

Three months passed since Tamar's disappearance from the house of Judah. Yet, when she reappeared, rumors surfaced that she was with child by whoredom. "Bring the whore to me!" demanded Judah. "Have her stand before me and the men of our community, that she giveth an accounting of herself, and withstandeth judgment for her sins." Simeon and Levi gathered the men of the tribe in a grand tribunal. Still wearing the blackened mourning garb of the widow, Tamar was fetched by guards. Tamar did not resist. In fact, she volunteered eagerly to stand in front of the tribunal, where she planned to present herself in public as the rebel, the vanguard for change, even though the punishment for harlotry could be death by fire.

Judah, presiding as judge and jury, proclaimed, "Tamar, daughter-in-law of my deceased son Er and then Onan, who died by your trickery and evil, ungodly ways, now stands unabashedly before us as the despicable whore who defiled our holy community and offended God All-Mighty. We demand to know the name of the perpetrator, so that he will burn with you as a sacrifice to appease God and a lesson to our women as to the consequence of whoredom."

Tamar stood boldly, proclaiming, "I do not recall the name of him with whom I layeth at the side of the road in Timnath, but he was an honorable man of high station. He took pity on me, for I, an outcast, was trapped in the role of the widow, falsely awaiting the son of the man, who was promised to me, but never delivered. For the sake of my freedom, I hath devised this trickery." Tamar revealed from under widow's garment the signet ring and staff, recognized by the entire community as Judah's missing property.

"Discern, I pray thee, men and women of our community." With that Tamar grasped the staff with whitened knuckles, raised it high, and pointed the staff at Judah, declaring with unfiltered vehemence, "You, sir, are my collaborator in sin. You, sir, are my partner in harlotry. You, sir, are my defiler. You, sir, make harlotry the only escape for women wishing freedom." A hush overpowered the congregation, as Judah, pierced and faltering in seeming defeat, slumped into his royal throne.

Instantly, Simeon rose to Judah's defense, weaving phrases as he spoke extemporaneously. "While it is true that Tamar carries Judah's child by the appearance of harlotry, in Truth Tamar's heartfelt intent was to seduce Judah for the sole purpose of continuing the lineage of the family of Judah. Isn't that right, my lord?"

While the congregation stirred with rumbling and confusion, Judah regained his composure, and retook the initiative. "It is true that I had been slow to offer Tamar my last son, Sheleah, for fear that he might meet the same fate of unjust death, as did his brothers, under the spell of this wicked woman. I pondered long and hard how to reconcile obligations to family lineage and the threat of God's curse in the hands of Tamar."

After a moment of reflection Judah continued, "I was swooning in desperate grief over the loss of my beloved wife, so I was vulnerable to the siren's song. Agreed. But now I recognize that Tamar was so sincerely committed to her place in my family, more than anything else, that she was willing to disguise herself and play the part of the harlot, so that I might unwittingly provide her with my seed, in place of Sheleah. I must judge that this was at the heart of her plan. I confess that she hath been more righteous than I. There hath been no harlotry herein. The placing of my seed in Tamar, however the circumstances, is my right, privilege, and obligation as the patriarch of my family and lord of my lineage."

All agreed that Tamar's life would be spared, but she was banished to the isolated outskirts of the village to live out her life with Judah's twin children, where she remained invisible to the women of the community.

Epilogue

Tamar birthed her twins in a highly unconventional manner. As was the custom of the community, the child who appears first was privileged. At the moment of birth, a string was attached to the hand of the firstborn, in order to distinguish the privileged one from the second, the servant child. Tamar's labor brought forth the first child, who received the string, but then the child suddenly retreated back into the womb behind the veil of uncertainty of the unborn. Then the child without the mark of distinction surged forward and entered the world first. Confusion reigned as to who was to be the privileged one by birth, and who was to be the servant by rule of birth order.

Dinah's apparition appeared to Tamar again, commenting, "Wouldn't it be just like you, Tamar, to bring into this world that which shatters the conventions, the rules of privilege through lineage, and issue in a 'world of equals.' But let me ask you this, Tamar: Will you train these equals to act in the ways of men, known for their claims to divine rights and lineage, violently seeking power over the Others, and studied in the art of trickery, deception, subjugation, and subterfuge? Or will you train them to play the part of the victim, the harlot, in order to shame and manipulate men to gain dominance over them to your ends, as women ignored and invisible?

"Or will you do things differently, Tamar? Or will you do things differently?"

The End

THE RIDDLE OF THE MAPLE TREE

In the shadow of a great maple tree,
whose muscular boughs and green leafy fingers
strain skyward to grasp the heavens,
stood Death,
hunched over,
laboring to rake the rotting leaves,
that inevitably litter the ground.

Rustling in the twilight of resignation,
lay a brittle, elderly soul, who,
with brown skeletonic fingers skittering,
claws against Fate as unjust and untimely.

In Spring,
young leaves entertain intoxicating visions
of ascension,
elevated and exhilarated
by the robust boughs
of Summer.
By Autumn,
wilting, wrinkled, wasted and withered,
hanging on.
In Winter,
despised by root, trunk, and bough
for sucking sustenance
from the impatient buds and flowers of Spring.

Legacies swoon and fall like fragile rotting leaves,
some perchance to nourish the roots,

like fruit, long after the planter's days are spent.
But most to simply fill the dust bins of
the forgotten,
like a falling rock that vanishes into a pond,
but creates no ripple.
A riddle
never pondered by the young green leaves
blindly soaring skyward.

The End